AF612513

DEATH DIGGERS HANDBOOK THREE

DIVINE DECAY

Copyright 2021 Stacey Rourke

Special thanks to:
Melissa Stevens (The Illustrated Author Design Services)
Melissa Ringsted (There For You Editing)
Stacy Sanford

All rights reserved. Published by Anchor Group Publishing. No part of this book may be reproduced or transmitted in any form or by any means, electronic or mechanical, including photocopying, recording, or by any information storage and retrieval system, without written permission from the publisher.

Find a full list of Stacey Rourke's books here:
www.staceyrourke.com

PLAYLIST TO ACCOMPANY EACH CHAPTER

Chapter One- "The Hide and Seek Song" Ready or Not OST
https://youtu.be/pKmTMrsfUWQ
Chapter Two- "All the Things She Said" by Tatu
https://youtu.be/ujpvNvSgcic
Chapter Three- "Would I Lie to You?" by Eurythmics
https://youtu.be/Uhpu2N4rQZM
Chapter Four- "Brutal" by Olivia Rodrigo
https://youtu.be/hM2U8cb8lhI
Chapter Five- "Mr. Bad Guy" by Freddie Mercury
https://youtu.be/ePJ-THG3KcI
Chapter Six- "Somebody's Watching Me" by Rockwell
https://youtu.be/7YvAYIJSSZY
Chapter Seven- "Cruel" by Chloe Adams
https://youtu.be/4NZJh8oBmOc
Chapter Eight- "Dog Days are Over" by Florence & the Machine
https://youtu.be/cIXQjSo4GCE
Chapter Nine- "I Still Haven't Found What I'm Looking For" by U2
https://youtu.be/e3-5YC_oHjE
Chapter Ten- "Come as You Are" by Nirvana
https://youtu.be/vabnZ9-ex7o
Chapter Eleven- "The Boys are Back In Town" by Thin Lizzy
https://youtu.be/nN120kCiVyQ
Chapter Twelve- "Sans and Papyrus Song" by JT Music
https://youtu.be/6cx1WaoWQ34

Chapter Thirteen- "Know Who You Are" written by Lin-Manuel Miranda

https://youtu.be/sf3CevfP-E8

Chapter Fourteen- "Without Me" by Eminem

https://youtu.be/YVkUvmDQ3HY

Chapter Fifteen- "Living Dead Girl" by Rob Zombie

https://youtu.be/BvsMPOfblfg

Chapter Sixteen- "Game of Survival" by Ruelle

https://youtu.be/-T5eYF9WiRI

Chapter Seventeen- "Pretty Woman" by Roy Orbison

https://youtu.be/3KFvoDDs0XM

Chapter Eighteen- "Moonlight Sonata" by Beethoven

https://youtu.be/4Tr0otuiQuU

&

"Father and Son" by Cat Stevens

https://youtu.be/ZxjTC0bmKls

Chapter Nineteen- "Some Nights" by Fun

https://youtu.be/qQkBeOisNM0

&

"Thriller" by Michael Jackson

https://youtu.be/sOnqjkJTMaA

Chapter Twenty- "Galway Girl" by Ed Sheeran

https://youtu.be/87gWaABqGYs

Chapter Twenty-One- "Rhiannon" Piano Instrumental by Fleetwood Mac

https://youtu.be/8r8HsQjgPU0

&

"Love Me Like There's No Tomorrow" by Freddie Mercury

https://youtu.be/H1Wbu_AF2e4

Oh, and…

"Total Eclipse of the Heart" by Bonnie Tyler

https://youtu.be/lcOxhH8N3Bo

OBLIVION SEA

MAP OF CARNAGE CROSSING

EXPIRATION ROUNDABOUT

LANE

CROAKING

NIGHTSHADE ALLEY

EXPIRATION ROUNDABOUT

EXPIRATION ROUNDABOUT

EXPIRATION ROUNDABOUT

LEGEND

1. CATASTROPHE THEATER
2. FUNERAL PYRE FLOWERS
3. DEATH SHROUD CLOTHING & MORE
4. MORTALITY ESTATES
5. HOME DEADPOT
6. DEAD END RESORT & DAY SPA
7. DR. DESPAIR
8. ETERNAL NIGHT FOREST
9. WORMS WART DAM
10. CLIFFS OF DESPAIR
11. WAKE THE DEAD COFFEE
12. HOLLOWS END APOTHECARY
13. THE SCREAMING WELL
14. AFTERLIFE CLUB
15. SIX FEET UNDER SQUARE

OBLIVION SEA

ONE

If I wanted to turn around—and I did—circumstances wouldn't allow it. Circumstances being the tight quarters of a concrete drainage tube and the surly pirate behind me urging me to quicken my pace.

On my hands and knees, I shuffled onward to Legba only knows where. "I mean, it doesn't make sense!" I sputtered for what had to be the umpteenth time. "The Rofenod—a hideous beast with a hand for a head and razor-sharp teeth in its eyeball—is my father? *My father*? The King everyone in Carnage Crossing loved and adored? How is that possible?"

Flicking a silvery-blond strand of hair from his eyes, Gideon Poe's ocean blue eyes peered my way from under his brow. "We were just shoved into a whiskey barrel escape hatch by a talking skeleton to escape your sister, who is armed with only a doll. It's safe to say we have entered new realms of the plausibly explainable."

Dirt and grime smudged his face, squishing between his fingers as he crawled after me. I was an equally filthy mess. That said, the need for a shower was the least of my worries. My kingdom of the dead was being overthrown by my dark-hearted sister, Charlie, who was in possession of the one thing no one in this macabre little oasis had… a pulse. Combine that with her extensive research into the occult and a creepy little voodoo doll, and she could turn any dead being into her unwilling puppet. Hence our fleeing.

You know that *peace* part of R.I.P? I had no idea where that was on the itinerary, but it seemed long overdue.

"Any idea where this tunnel ends?" Concern laced my tone for a good reason. I could hear water rushing up ahead. "If this whole place is going to flood, a little forewarning would be nice."

"I'm guessing we are somewhere near the dam. Once we make it out, we'll find a place to camp for the night. Come morning, we can set out in search of your father." Gideon paused for a moment to inspect a small slice on his palm. One of many, I'm sure.

"That *thing* is not my father!" I tried to glance back over my shoulder, only to smack my forehead on the side of the tunnel. "Do I need to remind you that it regularly attacks me? If there is any humanity left in that thing at all, it's buried way too deep to tap into."

Wiping his hand on the side of his pants, Gideon shuffled onward. "If you're referring to the Hollow's Eve Ball or the night at the theater, I'd like to remind you that Ambrose, your conniving ex, was present on both occasions. Perhaps he was attacking *that* manipulative rat, and not you."

Planting my hand in a moist, mildewy spot, I leaned far to the side just so I could glare in his direction. "Stop making excuses for the repulsive monster, of which I am no relation!"

Gideon blinked my way, allowing me to stew in the heavy silence.

"And don't you dare make any kind of *thou doth protest too much* comment," I tagged on for good measure.

"Your words, not mine." He let one shoulder rise and fall in a casual shrug. "While I completely understand your need to come to terms with this rather startling information on your own, I would like to point out that nothing good will happen if little sis catches up with us. She's familiar with the exorcism process, and that is a degree of dead no one I know of has made it back from. So, if we could move this along…" Gideon trailed off, letting me pick up on what he was laying down all on my own.

With a huff, I resumed by soggy trudge. "Fine, but—*ahhhhhh*!"

Whatever pointless threat or baseless ultimatum I was about to make morphed into a guttural scream as my hand slipped and plunged me head-first down a ninety-degree incline. Skin was scraped from bone by the rough tunnel walls. Bones crunched. My skull cracked against unforgiving concrete. Black spots danced before my eyes as I was spat out onto the ground below.

Glancing down, I groaned in annoyance at the three broken ribs protruding from my torso. Squeezing my eyes shut, I let my head fall back in the dirt. "Great; now they'll be stuck like that. *Hummmph*!"

I'd like to say I knew Gideon would soon be tumbling down after me and moved out of the way accordingly, but that was not the case. My broken bones were snapped back into place when he crashed down on top of me.

"Blimey!" Planting his hands on either side of my head, he eased his weight off of me. "Are you okay, *mo bhanrion?*"

Stare fixed on the green and purple lights of the Veil swirling across the skyline, for a beat the only response I could offer was a brief nod. "We really need to work on our date-night activities," I finally managed, gingerly poking at my cracked ribs. "One that doesn't involve monsters and extreme bodily harm."

"If a life absent of monsters is what you're after, allow me to be the bearer of bad news," a soft voice trilled.

Gideon leaped to his feet, the dagger at his hip finding its way into his hand.

The best I could do was roll onto my side with a wince and blink up at the shadowy silhouette. "If you're here to kill us, I can guarantee you're going to be disappointed."

The figure stepped out from behind a thick thatch of birch saplings. White eyes peered my way from beneath a thick woolen cloak. Skin kissed blue by death was accentuated by pale blonde hair cut into a flirty bob. "Death is not a victory, My Queen, but one of many outcomes I have foreseen."

Propping myself up onto one elbow, my shoulders sagged in relief. "Ember, as happy as I am to see you, now isn't the best time for one of your creepy rhymes."

Offering me a hand, she helped hoist me to my feet. "Actually, I come with a gift." Once I got my legs under me, she handed over the burlap sack hanging from her forearm.

As I accepted it, I glanced at Gideon and gave him a nod to lower his blade. "What is this? Something to help me fight Charlie? A bazooka would be nice. I have no idea how to use one, but even with the risk of blowing my own head off being a primary concern, I'm willing to give it a try." I riffled around in the bag until my fingers found something round with smooth ridges. "Or, you know, I could try to take her out with– *sweet mother of Hades*! It's a skull! It's Bones's skull! You brought me his head? *Why*? Why would you do that? *Is he okay*?"

Startled by the skull, I tossed it in the air where Gideon easily caught it. "It's a mask," he pointed out, turning it around so I could see the head-sized hole in the bottom.

Pushing back the hood of her cloak, Ember dipped her chin in a nod. "Made of paper mache, in fact. While it doesn't belong to Bones, he was the model. We made it for a *Dia de los Muertos* themed production Vesper did some time ago. Seeing how you need to hide in plain sight, it seemed something that would be of great use to you now."

I swallowed down the lump of dread lodged in my throat. "Then you know what's happening?"

Ember's gaze drifted skyward, her eyes closing as if reading the breeze caressing her skin. "Trees have returned to the barren forest. Vines are once more ripe with fruit. But the elements are unbalanced. The natural order is in a state of chaos. Make no mistake, there are always consequences when the living penetrate our world."

As if cued by the sentiment, a powerful gust of wind whipped through the valley we had landed in, bending the trees surrounding us in half.

"I'm guessing it has something to do with that." I pointed to the patchwork fissures in the Veil. From those cracks dark shadows seeped in, riding the winds to the farthest reaches of the island.

Ember's eyes popped open, her milky irises cleared to a brilliant azure. "A storm is building. One with a disastrous fury."

Extending my arm in Gideon's direction, I jerked my head in a gesture for the mask. After he placed it in my hand, I turned it over in cursory inspection. "And this is somehow going to help with that?"

The likeliness to Bones was uncanny; it was carved and painted with expert attention to detail. Thick black netting covered the eye sockets and behind the jaws, blocking out any glimpse of what lay beneath.

Ember rolled her wrist, watching as something intangible slipped through her fingers. "Webs of darkness surround your sister. It's just as I warned long ago; *the queen whose heart is darkened by the grave will make Carnage Crossing her tortured slave. Only by embracing the monstrous ferocity of love will the ruler we deserve rise above*. That time is now. It has begun. Everything you do from this point on will decide the fate of Carnage Crossing."

Gideon flipped his knife over the back of his hand and slid it back into its sheath. "You being a seer, do you have any information to help expedite a solution?"

Lips pressed in a thin line, she shook her head. "There are limitless possibilities with too many potential outcomes for me to get an accurate read on."

"Awesome." I clucked my tongue against the roof of my mouth and dragged my fingers through my hair. "Instead of helpful information, you brought me a head. As one does in times of uncertainty."

Leaves crunched under Ember's buckled shoes as she closed the distance between us, pressing in close enough for me to smell the cloves permeating her clothing. "Your sibling marched in to take what's yours. You're going to want to fight back. It's in your nature as a person… as a *queen*. While I cannot see where this journey ends, I can assure you of one thing: every outlook I see shows your eternal demise if you are caught by Charlie on her terms and not your own. For the sake of yourself—for the sake of us all—you must stay safely hidden until you've devised a way to stop her."

"I will," I croaked, my grip tightening on the mask.

Taking a step back, Ember's full-length skirt whispered around her ankles as she turned her attention to Gideon. "You care for her?"

"With all that I am, and all that I have," he confirmed without an ounce of hesitation.

"See to it that she holds true to her word." Flicking her hood back into place with a sharp snap of the fabric, Ember turned on her heel and began her march back to the city with determined strides.

"Ember!" I called after her, apprehension getting the best of me. "What's happening in town? Is everyone okay?"

She paused midstride. Keeping her back to me, Ember tipped her chin in my direction. "No. None of us are. And we won't be, as long as Charlie is in Carnage Crossing."

TWO

We made camp on an inlet on the south side of Worm's Wart Dam, where the newly restored foliage was thick enough to shield us from view. In no way did that put my mind at ease. Seated on a boulder with my gaze fixed on the campfire Gideon built, I rubbed my hands up and down my arms to fight off the chill resonating from my very soul.

Easing down beside me, Gideon wrapped his arms around me to lend what little warmth his embrace could provide. "You haven't uttered a word since Ember scurried off. What's running through your mind, *mo bhanrion?*"

Watching the fingers of flame lick towards the sky, I shook my head and tried to pinpoint the exact moment everything spiraled out of control.

"I don't know," I finally muttered, answering both his question and mine. "I have no idea what to do. Since I arrived here I've just trusted my gut and gone with what felt right. This time? Nothing about this feels good or bears any resemblance to right."

His voice soft with understanding, Gideon pulled me closer and rested his chin on the top of my head. "Why do you think that is?"

Shrugging out of the blissful comfort of his arms, I sprang to my feet and paced an agitated trail into the earth behind the fire. "Because she's my sister! Doesn't that make me somewhat responsible for unleashing her on the world? I mean, I lived with her for *years* and never knew she was capable of this level of depravity. Did I know she could be a bitch? Of course! Show me a person who says their sibling can't be a complete and total ass from time to time, and I'll tell you that person is a liar. But this? There is a Grand Canyon-sized difference between a snotty chick who can tear others down by pinpointing their insecurities, and a she-devil hellbent on enslaving an entire undead population! And I didn't see it. Granted, she wasn't skinning cats in the backyard or anything as obvious as that. Still, there had to be some sort of warning signs I missed."

Face vacant of judgment, Gideon kept his tone quiet and compassionate. "She's your sister. You love her. You never wanted to think her capable of this sort of malicious treachery."

Swiveling his way, I jammed my index finger in his direction. "See, that's a great sentiment in theory, but doesn't it make me an ostrich with my head in the sand? With all I thought I knew about her, I was completely blindsided by this."

"You are not an ostrich." One corner of Gideon's mouth tugged back in a hint of a smile he valiantly fought to suppress. "We never know what people are truly capable of, because they only show us the side of themselves they want us to see. Some can exhibit unparalleled acts of generosity or unimaginable heroics that leave us in awe. Others commit acts so vile it sickens us to speak of them. You didn't see atrocious, violent behavior and ignore it. Therefore, you are in no way to blame for her actions. You are two separate people with your own knowledge, goals, and insight. Neither of you can truly control the heart and mind of the other… no matter what talents she may have with that hideous little doll of hers."

My posture snapped ramrod straight as an idea brightened my eyes. "Gideon! You're a genius!"

"Always love to hear that, but why in this particular instance?"

"Charlie has information we don't… and so did my father. Both of them marked themselves with the protective eye. But why? What do they know that we don't?" Jogging back over to him, I shoved the cloak Bones gifted me to the side and thumbed open the top four buttons of my blouse beneath. Slipping the fabric off one shoulder, I crouched down in the dirt beside Gideon. "And that gives me an idea."

One brow hitched with interest, desire clouded Gideon's eyes to a deep shade of sapphire. His stare traveled down my neck and teased over my exposed clavicle. "I'm getting an idea all my own, but I doubt it's what you're hinting at."

"Take out your knife. I want you to mark me with the protective eye. Then, I'll do you." Wiggling my knees into the dirt, I got into a more comfortable position to brace myself for being permanently scarred.

Gideon's lips parted with a pop. "Yeah, that's not where I hoped this was going at all." With the side of one knuckle, he brushed the delicate skin under my jawline. "I had something far more tender in mind."

"And I love your enthusiasm for our long-awaited pelvic rumba. I do." Ignoring his chuckle, I rambled on in my long-winded explanation. "However, right now, my sister is trying to build an army of mindless puppets. If that mark has some sort of power, I want to know what it is. Come on; a little pain, a bit of black gore we're both going to pretend we don't see, and we may end up with some information we can actually use!"

Rolling onto one hip, Gideon pulled his knife from its sheath. "Just when I think I'm starting to understand you, you ask me to stab you." Flipping the blade over the back of his hand, he offered it to me by the hilt. "That said, I'm not entirely sure what this design is supposed to look like. I'll trust you to go first, My Queen, by carving it onto me. Then, I will replicate it to the best of my ability."

Tugging his linen shirt over his head, he tossed it aside and presented me with the full gloriousness of his bare chest. Sculpted pecs. Rippling abs. The deep V of his hips that muddled all coherent thought. Another time, different circumstances, and I would have taken full advantage of our long-desired alone time. Now, we had far more pressing matters at hand.

"I know we don't feel pain like the living, but I am sorry. This is going to sting." Biting back my regret, I sliced the point of the blade into his grey-hued skin.

Gideon winced, yet didn't pull away as I carved out the design by memory. Tissue parted in shallow divots, allowing inky black ooze to seep from the cuts. Tearing off the bottom hem of my shirt, I used it to wipe the wounds clean so I could see the next mark I needed to make. Little by little I etched until the protective eye—in its entirety—was carefully imprinted over Gideon's stilled heart. Patting the mark clean, I inspected my work.

"There you go. I either gave you a useful tool, or a permanent piece of body adornment nowhere near as pretty as your other one." I tapped the pirate ship tattoo on his shoulder as I referenced it. "I'll go clean the blade and you can do mine." Pushing to my feet, I walked to a small spring that had been carved out by the spray of the dam. Dipping the blade in, I erased all traces of the gore that marked it.

I could feel the heat of Gideon's stare on me, my back tingling under the intensity of his gaze. Stretching one leg out in front of him, he propped the opposite foot on the boulder and laced his fingers around his knee. "Tell me, My Queen, what exactly is the plan once we're done branding one another?"

Turning the knife in one direction then the other, I studied how the green and purple lights of the Veil glimmered off its blade. "Well, Bones was insistent that I track down the Rofenod and confront him, but I have no idea how that interaction would even go. What do I say? *Hey, freaky hand monster, rumor has it you're my dad. Please confirm by shrieking once for yes and twice for no.*"

As I rose to my full height and shook the excess water from the knife, Gideon offered me a charming half-smile. "I doubt it would happen quite that way."

"No, in reality, there would probably be a great deal more terrified whimpering on my part. Even so, I have another idea… but you're not going to like it." Dropping to my knees beside him, I offered him the hilt of the blade.

"Even more than I despise stabbing the woman I love?"

"Most definitely."

"So far, not feeling good whatever it is you're hinting at."

I bit the inside of my cheek as Gideon brought the knife to my skin and made the first cut. "Remember the *one* thing Ember told me to do?"

With firm yet gentle strokes, Gideon carved out the Hamsa hand. "To stay hidden, or face certain exorcism? Yes, a message like that is rather hard to forget."

"What if…" Hard to say if my grimace was caused by the knife digging into my flesh or the suggestion it pained me to make. "… Instead of doing that, we march right back into the heart of town?"

Gaze flicking to my face, Gideon lifted the point of the blade. "And why, in Legba's name, would we even consider doing that?"

"We need to know what this does, right?" I nodded towards the handiwork he was slicing into the rise of my left breast. "We aren't going to find that out here, in the middle of nowhere. If we're going to test it out, we need to be right in the middle of this chaotic mess."

Wetting his lips, Gideon chose his words carefully. "And what if it's some sort of homing beacon that leads Charlie right to you? Like a supernatural sonar?"

Tucking a lock of hair behind my ear, I shook my head. "I don't think it is. Bones said my father drew the mark on my mother to protect her when she got sick. There has to be a reason why. If it *is* some sort of ward of protection, we owe it to our people to try it out and arm them with it."

Bowing his head to his task once more, Gideon etched out the line for the fourth finger. "And if I told you I thought this plan was completely ludicrous and an unnecessary risk?"

"I'd say you're absolutely right, but I need to do it anyway."

"Will you wear the mask she gave you?"

Catching his hand, I gave it a tight squeeze of enthusiasm. "Does that mean you'll go with me?"

Chin falling to his chest, he sighed and glanced up at me from under his thick lashes. "Will you wear the sodding mask?"

Despite having never been a girl scout, I held up their three-fingered salute. "Not only will I wear it, but I'll also zip my lips so no one has any idea it's me." Seeing his shoulders sag with defeat, I fished for my answer. "So, you won't fight me on this? We can venture back into the heart of the city?"

Finishing my mark, Gideon stabbed the point of the blade into the dirt. "*Mo bhanrion*, I discovered shortly after meeting you that fighting anything you have your heart set on is a losing battle. Though I do insist we take every precaution possible, gather the information we need, and get out as quickly as we can."

Throwing myself at him, I grabbed Gideon in a fierce koala bear hug—which would have been a sweeter gesture if my chest wasn't oozing sludge. "Thank you so much! We'll be in and out before you know it!"

It seemed a simple plan with little room for error. Of course, it went tragically wrong.

THREE

The narrow eye sockets of the mask made it mandatory for me to keep my stare locked on the ground to avoid tripping over my own feet. But it worked. With Gideon by my side, I was able to stride into town and meld with the buzzing crowd without being noticed. Though why everyone was out, filling the streets and exchanging nervous whispers was a mystery that was solved the instant I heard Charlie's voice booming out from Six Feet Under Square.

Careful to stay hidden, Gideon and I snaked along the back of the crowd gathering at the steps of the stone gazebo to listen to her with curious interest.

Hands on her hips, Charlie paced from one side of the gazebo to the other wearing an outfit that looked like an eighties-fashion-meets-S&M fever dream. "In time," she crowed, "you may come to appreciate my presence here. And why wouldn't you? I've brought back life, new growth, and your only means of food. Still, in the interest of complete transparency, you should know that's far from my primary goal. I plan to assert myself as the ultimate ruler over Carnage Crossing, molding and shaping this realm into something that far exceeds even my father's wildest expectations… melding the worlds of the living and the dead in ways never before thought possible."

The residents gave snorts of disbelief, rolling their eyes at the audacity of the newcomer.

My sister's heartbeat quickened in a pulsating warning that echoed all around. Her eyes darkened with challenge, words leaving her lips in an ominous hiss. "You will all bend the knee before me… just as soon as you realize you have no other choice."

"I don't like the sound of that," I forced the words through clenched teeth, my nostrils flaring beneath my mask.

Glancing to her right, Charlie lifted her chin. A line of bodies shuffled up onto the gazebo behind her and a fist of fear squeezed around the cold lump of my heart. These weren't just any random residents. They were the brave line of defense that stood against Charlie while I made my escape from the resort.

Lugosi.

Mel.

Malaria.

Azrael.

Sparrow.

Bones.

Shoulders slumped, eyes vacant and glassy, they ambled into a line behind Charlie to await her further command.

Throwing her arms out in an exaggerated shrug, her lips curled into a vindictive smile. "You don't know me. I'm just some chick with great hair and an ass that won't quit who sauntered in here demanding loyalty. Truth be told, I'd judge you all horribly if you blindly obliged. You need convincing, I get that. How about a little show and tell?"

"This is not going to end well," Gideon muttered in a barely audible whisper.

Boots scuffing against the concrete floor of the gazebo, Charlie sauntered to Sparrow's side. My lady-in-waiting's gaze remained frozen straight ahead while Charlie pinched Sparrow's chin between her thumb and forefinger.

"This brave little pixie rushed me when I arrived. How about if we start with her?" Flinging Sparrow's head to the side with more force than necessary, Charlie took a step back and pulled her voodoo doll from the pocket of her coat of a thousand zippers. Stare locked on Sparrow, she removed the pin from the doll's forehead and gave my icy blonde friend her free will back.

The instant Sparrow's eyes blinked into focus, she unleashed an enraged scream and lunged for Charlie's throat.

She didn't lay a finger on her.

Not even close.

Sparrow barely made it half a stride before Charlie stabbed the pin into the stomach of her doll. Battle cry morphing into a scream of anguish, Sparrow crumbled to the ground. Inky black sludge gushed from the fresh wound in her torso, pooling around her in a growing crimson slick.

Seemingly oblivious to Sparrow's ability to feel pain, Charlie sloshed through the spraying gore. Glaring down at her helpless victim, my sister pinched the head of the pin and wriggled it from side to side. "Get on your knees."

Stifling her yelps of pain, Sparrow fumbled to get legs under her, slipping in her own staled blood along the way.

"Very good," Charlie purred. "Now, look at me."

The onlookers had all fallen silent, equal parts fear and outrage sizzling through the crowd in a palpable current.

With black-tinged tears streaming down her cheeks and dripping from her chin, Sparrow did as directed.

"Who am I?" Charlie's tone may have been sugary sweet, but the look in her eye was that of a predator on the hunt.

Sparrow tried to shake her head, denying the words Charlie meant to force from her lips. Her weak efforts widened my sister's smile, causing her to grind the pin in deeper still.

"*The Queen*! You are the Queen!" Unable to withstand a second more of the torture, Sparrow slumped forward onto her elbows.

"Good girl." Charlie patted Sparrow's head, then plunged the pin back between the eyes of her doll, returning my lady-in-waiting to a state of mindless servitude. "As you can see, all I need is to focus my attention on any one of you and you'll become my next plaything. Try and fight it. I dare you. It won't matter in the slightest. One way or another, *all* of you will bow before me."

I wanted to rush the stage. To rip that doll from her hands and smack the shit out of her with it. Experience had taught me what would happen if I tried. She would torture me just as she had in the kitchen of the townhouse, but this time all of Carnage Crossing would be watching. They would see their queen broken and bloody at the hands of another, and all hope would be lost. If I held any chance of saving us all, I had no choice but to stay hidden long enough to figure out how.

One glance around—my mask wobbling at the motion—was all it took to see I wasn't the only one having a difficult time digesting Charlie's forceful intrusion. Hands were curled into tight fists. Faces were set in stern masks of rage. And I wasn't the only one who noticed.

Rogue curls haloed Charlie's head as she leveled her glare at the first row of people in front of her. Focus locked on them, she stabbed the pin into the back of her doll's leg. A wave of bodies crashed to the ground, their legs suddenly buckling beneath them.

"Is that enough?" Charlie asked, her tone mocking faux innocence. "Or should I keep going?" A sweeping glance at the second row, and she crippled them in the same fashion.

Some around me looked ready to run.

Others took preemptive measures and dropped to their knees.

Neither option mattered. Intoxicated by the power she possessed, Charlie scanned the sea of faces before her for the next to feel her wrath. Then… hesitated. Something that resembled doubt flashed across her features.

Clearing her throat, she tossed her hair back from her face. "In the words of Chris Evans, my future baby-daddy, in his iconic role as Captain America, *I can do this all day*. But it would be so much more fulfilling for me to see you all kneel on your own. If for no other reason than to simply not see more of your friends in pain."

And there it was.

Three rapid blinks while she picked at the cuticle of her pinkie finger with her thumb.

My sister's tell.

"She's lying," I whispered out of the corner of my mouth. "She can't stretch her power out any further than that."

Gideon's head snapped in my direction, fires of purpose burning behind his eyes. "Are you sure?"

"No, I didn't spill marinara sauce on the shirt you loaned me."

"Of course I didn't tell Mom it was you who dented the car door."

"Your boyfriend tried to kiss me, *Thadia. Not the other way around."*

All those years growing up together.

Countless, seemingly insignificant fibs.

Each time I learned the truth because of her unmistakable tell.

"I'm positive."

"Good," Gideon grumbled, his chest puffed with determination. "Stay here."

As he stepped forward, I seized his arm and held him back. "What? Where are you going?"

Seas of rage stormed in the depths of his ocean blue eyes the instant his stare met mine. "You want answers? I'm going to go get them for you."

Before I could argue further, he pulled his arm from my grasp and marched straight for the gazebo, shoving people out of his way and stepping over those who had voluntarily lowered themselves before Charlie. To my absolute horror, my pirate beau purposely made a spectacle of himself as he closed in fast on my psychotic little sis.

Watching him approach, Charlie's lips twisted to the side in taunting amusement. "Aw, are you not convinced yet, hot stuff? Think you're man enough to withstand the pain and take me out? By all means, step right up!"

Attention locked on Gideon, she slid the pin from the doll and waited. To others, it may have appeared she was giving him a chance to reconsider and back down, but I saw the truth for what it was. Charlie didn't attempt to cast out her influence over him until he was roughly ten feet away from her.

Only then did she drive the pin into the back of her doll's leg hard and fast.

Gideon stopped.

Stiffened.

Then bowed his head and drove his knee down into the earth.

My theory was right. Her power had strict limits.

Wearing a cat-who-ate-the-canary grin, Charlie peered out at the subjugated mass. "That was exciting, wasn't it?" She giggled, flicking her tongue over the tip of one incisor. "I suppose one of you needed to try that out to see what would happen, but I hope the rest of you see that as the learning experience it was. Next time, I'll be far less forgiving. Now, back to business. Who is… Lugosi?"

Silence.

No one moved.

Blinked.

Shifted.

Clucking her tongue against the roof of her mouth, Charlie rolled her eyes. "It's adorable that you think not answering is an option. I have no problem picking out random folks and using my needle to loosen their tongues until someone spills the truth."

Despite being a puppet to Charlie's will, Lugosi shuffled forward a half-step and gave a gruff grunt.

"Look at that! A volunteer." Stabbing her pin into the head of the doll, she pulled it right back out, freeing him to speak. "Do you know who this Lugosi is?"

Mel made a guttural sound of warning that Lugosi quieted by raising one hand. "That's me. I'm Lugosi."

Eyes narrowing, she let her gaze travel the length of him. The gothically fabulous ensemble. That spiky green hair. Expertly applied guy-liner that achieved the perfect smoky-eyed look. "You're the man I talked to through the Ouija board before my sister died?"

"I am," he croaked, wetting his lips.

"Well, then." One shoulder lifting in a resigned shrug, Charlie traced her thumb over the doll's worn burlap. "It seems we have a wedding to plan."

"We do?" Brow furrowed, Lugosi glanced Mel's way in confusion.

Mel tried to shake his head, yet could only manage a twitch under Charlie's stifling hold.

"Yes, silly!" Charlie swatted at the air between them. "You told me that the Hand and the Queen had to unite to secure my reign. That's you and me, sweet cheeks."

Bless his long-cold heart, Lugosi couldn't suppress a cringe. "Oh, *that*. How do I put this? *That* was a big misunderstanding. We tried it out when your sister arrived and it served no purpose whatsoever. So… no need for us to pick out china patterns or fight over who gets to wear the veil."

All forms of pleasantries vanished in a blink, and Charlie's pupils dilated with a murderous gleam. "Really? What a convenient thing to say now that I'm here and standing in front of you."

Mel gave a huff of warning and managed a step closer to his love.

Shaking his head, a lock of bright green hair fell across Lugosi's forehead and tangled in his lashes. "I'm speaking solely on past experience. It was completely unnecessary. Not to mention, I don't think I'd be the ideal husband for you. In case literally *everything* about me didn't clue you in, I'm gay. So, not exactly the *best* choice for the Queen's Consort."

Head tilted, her glare shot daggers of ice his way. "I didn't ask if you wanted to fall in love. I'm merely requesting you honor your word and play the part required of you for me to take the crown. To say I'd be unhappy if you stood in the way of my succession would be a vast understatement. Truthfully, I just don't know how

I would vent my frustration…" Letting that threatening sentiment hang in the air between them, Charlie cast a pointed glance in Mel's direction.

Heartbreak etched into his features, Lugosi bit the inside of his cheek and forced himself to meet Charlie's glower. "Leave him out of this, and I will fulfill my obligations as the former Hand of the King."

"Fantastic." Even as she offered him a tight smile, the sentiment was in no way reflected in the sharp and cunning look in her eyes. "But I *do* think I'll keep your friend close by. We'll call it motivation… just in case." A snap of her fingers called Sparrow and Bones to action. "Take them to the manor. Lock them in separate rooms, then guard the doors to make sure they are on their very best behavior."

They hobbled off, Mel and Lugosi reluctantly in tow, while those of us left behind waited for the second shoe to drop. No way was this over. Not yet.

We didn't have to wait long for Charlie to tick off the next item on her agenda. With only Malaria and Azrael left in her little toy box, Charlie sauntered behind them and threw an arm around their shoulders. "As for you two, my sister is still out there… somewhere. I need you to find her for me. If anyone gets in your way or tries to stop you, tear them limb from limb and toss the pieces into the sea." Turning on the heel of her platform boot, Charlie made it to the stairs of the gazebo before stopping to tag on, "Oh, and feel free to use whatever force is necessary. If all you can deliver is her head, present it on a silver platter."

With that, she stomped off toward the manor, leaving the confused crowd buzzing in her wake.

"Safe to say we won't be doing family Christmas this year," I grumbled to myself as I shoved my way through bodies in my mad dash to Gideon. Clasping a hand onto his forearm, I helped guide him to his feet. "Are you okay? What were you thinking? That was so reckless! She could have—"

I trailed off when I noticed Gideon's shoulders shaking with humorless laughter. Seizing hold of my arm, he pulled me closer and whispered against my ear, "The mark works, Tempest. I faked the entire thing. It protected me from her influence."

FOUR

Key in the lock, Gideon threw his shoulder into the door of Funeral Pyre Flowers to pop it open. Life had returned to his shop to a smothering degree. Ivy grew up the walls and braided across the floor. Fruit trees exploded with produce, their ripe offerings falling from laden branches. Flowers and foliage of every kind swelled into enormous sprays through which Gideon had to draw his knife and slice us a path.

Mask off and cradled under my arm, I stayed close to his side as we weaved our way through the monstrous greenery. "Why exactly did we need to make a pitstop here? Are we hoping a lovely arrangement will sway Charlie's twisted agenda? Because the only chance that plan has is the possibility of aggravating her allergies."

"We need to disappear. To get far from little sister's reach and come up with a plan that doesn't involve lingering right under her nose and praying she doesn't notice us." Reaching a cedar wardrobe closet, Gideon creaked open its doors. He snatched a satchel from a shelf within and opened it to examine the contents. "Knife. Matches. Blanket. Empty canteen. You grab some fruit and vegetables, I'll fill the canteen, and we'll have everything we need to run."

Plucking apples, oranges, and pears from the bountiful trees, I took Gideon's frantic sense of urgency into mind and chose my words carefully. "We just learned of a pretty damned potent tool to use against Charlie. Why would we run now?"

"Because it isn't enough." Gideon tightened the lid on the canteen and shoved its sloshing contents into the satchel. "It's a shield we can hide behind, but not the sword we need to cut off the head of the beast—metaphorically speaking."

Keeping my tone calm and measured, I handed him the fruit, noticing how his skin brushed mine as he accepted it. "What is it you think we should do?"

Stowing away the produce, he flung the stocked satchel over his shoulder. "Azrael and Malaria are hunting for you. I say we hang back long enough to mark them so they can start freeing others from Charlie's will. Then, we climb aboard my ship and sail around the island in search of the Rofenod—as we promised Bones we would. The upside is that at least out on the water, no one can sneak up on us."

"This is probably the part where you expect me to argue."

"Without a doubt."

"Not today. We need a plan, and that's a hard thing to come up with when you're running in fear of being wiped from existence."

Chin tucked to his chest, Gideon's nose crinkled in disbelief. "Really? Because I had a whole argument planned to convince you."

"Ah, shoot. That would have been fun." Sweeping my arm in front of me, I snapped my fingers in mock dismay. "How about if we focus those powers of persuasion on figuring out how to draw Azrael and Malaria to us?"

Adjusting his hold on the bag, Gideon lifted one muscular shoulder in a shrug. "Malaria seems to come running whenever you commit any sort of fashion faux pas. Maybe put on those shoes with the big buckles you think go with everything and she'll sniff you out."

For a beat, I blinked in his direction. "That was more hurtful than helpful."

"That's Malaria," he offered, as if that excused his comment in any way.

Further conversation was cut off by the back door of the shop exploding open with a force that snapped one of its hinges in two. As kindling flew and debris rained down, an ear-piercing shriek echoed through the shop. Two silhouettes filled the doorway, their postures tense and poised for battle.

Clapping his hands over his ears, Gideon squinted through the cloud of dust settling. "Who is that?"

Pushing a branch aside, I could make out waves of dark, side-swept hair. "Not to sound redundant, but… that's Malaria."

His fashion-related comment still fresh in my mind, the saucy pirate let his gaze flick down to the form-hugging leggings and off-the-shoulder peasant top hidden beneath my cloak. "I mean… the ensemble seems quite fetching to me."

"Smartass," I muttered to myself and took a step closer to the newly arrived twosome. "Malaria, I don't know if you're under Charlie's influence right now, but you and I both know the last thing you would want is someone making you their bitch. Thankfully, I know how to fix that. I won't lie, it's going to sting. But that's a small price to pay to get your free will ba—*aacccccck*!" My helpful suggestion turned into a yelp as Malaria grabbed an apple tree by the roots and whipped it at me.

While Gideon and I ducked in time to avoid being clobbered, the same couldn't be said for the neatly lined rows of herbs growing in planters on the table behind us. The smell of wet dirt filled the shop as soil pelted down in heavy clumps.

Seizing hold of my wrist, Gideon pulled me in the direction of the front door. "Tempest, look at them."

The haze of dust and dirt cleared, giving me the first glimpse of their macabre makeunders. "Oh… no," I muttered in a choked whisper. "Charlie… what have you done?"

The skin on the burned half of Malaria's face appeared freshly torched, her complexion blackened like charred meat. Meanwhile, Azrael's shroud had been ripped away, allowing a hypnotic galaxy to swirl in the depths of his hollowed socket. No light or life reflected from his other eye. Both had been reduced to mindless puppets… and nothing more.

Scrambling in a frantic backpedal, I let Gideon guide me to the nearest exit. "Just a wild guess here, but I don't think reasoning with them is an option right now."

"The zombie look doesn't exactly say *compelling conversationalist*, now does it?" Moving the strap of the satchel into a cross-body position, Gideon pulled out his pocket knife and flicked it open. "Got your mask? The second I get that door open, we're making a mad dash to the forest."

With two knuckles, I knocked on the top of my faux skull. "Got it. Think we can make it there before they reach us?"

Malaria and Azrael stalked closer, their heads tilted at inhuman angles as their taut muscles prepared for attack.

"To the forest?" Brows knitted tightly, Gideon shook his head. "Hell no. But out in the open, we'll have more space to fight them off."

Emerald wisps crackled down my arms as I watched Malaria take a threatening step forward. "That was in no way reassuring."

"It wasn't meant to be." At my side, my pirate beau laced his fingers with mine and gave a firm squeeze. Chest puffed in full protective bravado, he uttered one simple word against my ear. "Run."

Holding my mask tight to my chest, I swiveled as he did, both of us sprinting like the devil—or a pissed-off fashion designer—was chasing us.

Malaria was the first to launch into an attack. Legs pumping like pistons, she closed in with remarkable speed for someone sprinting in stilettos.

"*What in Legba's name*? Was that girl a track star in life?" I hollered, knocking an avocado tree down in front of her in the hopes of slowing her down.

Gideon slammed into the door with his shoulder, his free hand fiddling to free the lock. "Don't look back! Just move!"

"I would love to! *Now hurry up and open the door before she eats my head*!" As far as compelling counterpoints go, I felt mine was a stellar one.

The door clicked open, spilling us both out onto the street. Unfortunately, our momentary victory proved to be short-lived. While Malaria continued her bee-line straight for us, Azrael streaked down the side of the shop and burst through the front window with a deafening crash. Seemingly oblivious to the shards of glass embedded in his flesh, he landed in a low crouch and slowly rose to his full height.

With the forest as our goal, we were blocked in.

One of them in front of us.

The other behind.

That left just one option.

Fight.

Moving slowly and cautiously, I unbuttoned Gideon's satchel and dropped my mask inside. "Whatever is coming, I have a feeling I'm going to need both hands."

Pocketknife posed out in front of him, Gideon's nostrils flared. "Take out the other knife… and the rope."

Doing as he asked, I kept them close at my sides, unsure what the next possible step could be. "Do we have a plan? Or are we completely winging this?"

"We don't want to hurt them, just hold them still long enough to mark them." Eyebrows disappearing into his hairline, he took the rope from my hand and offered me a shrug. "So, yes, we are absolutely winging it. I'll keep Rocket Man busy. You handle Malaria."

"How am I supposed to do that?" I shrieked, panic bubbling through my tone.

Jogging backwards into the street, my pirate tossed me a wink. "I don't know. Talk fashion. Stop her from ripping out your throat with her teeth. You know, girlie stuff." With that, he spun around, gave a loud whistle, and broke into a jog across Nightshade Alley. "Oy! Over here, mate!"

Azrael wasted no time chasing after him, making surprisingly good time for someone who looked like an extra from *The Walking Dead*. Unfortunately, I couldn't watch what transpired between them. Not with Malaria on the prowl behind me. Teeth gnashing, she stalked a slow circle around me.

Adjusting my grip on the knife, I moved with her, unwilling to take my eyes off her for an instant. "I know we've had our differences, Malaria. Me being a person of compassion and decency, and you being the emotional equivalent of stepping on a Lego. But I like to think we've come to a common ground where we could get along. I have to say, that's going to change if you try to do something icky… like bite me."

Malaria's head tilted, the motion causing a scorched hunk of flesh to flake from her chin and fall away to expose her jaw bone beneath.

Swallowing hard, I stifled a cringe. "Girl, we have *got* to break you out of Charlie's influence. It does *not* look good on you."

Turns out even zombie-brain Malaria was immeasurably vain. Enraged by my insult, her jaw unhinged as she bellowed a ghastly shriek and tore straight for me. As her forearms slammed into my chest, instinct told me to grab on and keep distance inserted between us as we both went crashing to the ground.

The instant my shoulder blades made contact with the sidewalk, I threw my weight to the side. Rolling on top of her, I pinned her beneath me with my knees on either side of her torso.

Teeth gnashing, Malaria bucked and lurched beneath me, manic to be free. "This next part is going to be unpleasant. I'll apologize later… if it works." Lifting my knee, I wrestled her wrist under it and used my weight to hold her arm still. Her shrieks and thrashing reached a fevered pitch as I ripped open her sleeve and began carving the Hamsa hand into her upper arm.

Things were moving along nicely, the design almost finished when out of the corner of my eye I saw Gideon skidding across the ground on his back. Attention whipping in that direction, I watched in awe as the swoon-worthy pirate lassoed Azrael's ankle with the rope, then jumped up and ran four-wide strides in the opposite direction to cinch his knot tightly. With his legs suddenly forced together, zombie-Azrael halted his pursuit and resorted to frantic windmill arms to keep himself upright. With gravity working in his favor, Gideon jogged up behind Azrael and delivered a swift kick to the middle of his back. With a muffled yelp, the concierge tumbled head-first over the stone ledge of the Screaming Well. As his screams echoed up from below, Gideon looped the remaining rope around the spigot on the side and fastened it in a firm knot that prevented Azrael from crashing to the deep floor of the well.

Leaving the rope swaying and Azrael swinging upside down, Gideon brushed off his hands and turned my way. "He'll be occupied for a bit; how are things on your end?"

In typical Malaria fashion, she decided to answer for me in the rudest way possible. Which, in this case, meant headbutting me in the face. Cartilage cracked, spots danced before my eyes, and black sludge streaked from my nostrils.

"Been better," I grunted, wiggling my nose to determine if it was broken.

One final glance down at Azrael to ensure he was okay, then Gideon dashed over to help by pinning Malaria's shoulders to the ground. "I know I can be quite dashing," he winked, "but I didn't mean to distract you from the task at hand."

Not wasting a minute longer, I put my blade to work once more. "You're hot, and I have the attention span of a gnat. We're lucky I didn't let her run off while I sat here applauding how your butt looks in those pants."

Malaria kicked and screamed her annoyance until the outline of the design was finally sliced into her flesh. Only then did coherency seep back into her eyes and the more ghoulish attributes of her forced façade faded.

Which, of course, brought her attitude roaring back. "Are you about done? These cobblestones are putting creases in this blouse from which there will be no coming back. The torn fabric I can work with, unnatural pleats I cannot."

Taking the handkerchief Gideon offered from his back pocket, I wiped Malaria's arm clean before climbing to my feet and offering her a hand up. "You're welcome, by the way, for putting you back in control of your senses."

Accepting my help up, she rolled her eyes and brushed the dirt from the back of her pants. "Yes, of course. Thank you. A thousand times thank you for stepping up and doing the job you were entrusted with when you put on the crown."

Dragging my tongue over my top teeth, I glanced to Gideon. "If I cut the mark back off of her, can we give her back to Charlie? Because I could just hack off her arm."

Gideon said nothing, instead throwing his hands in the air to signify he would be playing the neutral part of Switzerland in this matter.

"As much as I love our incessant banter, I would suggest you hide yourself in some way." The dark waves of Malaria's hair brushed across her shoulder blades as she scanned the intersection between Nightshade Alley and Croaking Lane. "After your sister's power trip, I have no doubt most residents are hiding in their homes and barring the doors. Still, all it takes is one person seeing you, and Charlie will coax the information out of them in the most agonizing ways imaginable."

Gideon seconded that notion by pulling my mask out of his satchel and tossing it to me.

Catching it with one hand, I balanced the paper mache skull between my knees long enough to twist my hair up on top of my head before stuffing it back on. "Not a word," I warned Malaria as a smug smile twisted at the corners of her lips.

"Normally, I would have a million comments about what an improvement that is and how ashamed I am that I didn't think of this option for you first," she smirked. "But I'll spare you, considering it's a necessity."

Jabbing my hands onto my hips, the skull mask wobbled as I tilted my head. "Gee, thanks. That would have really sucked to hear."

"While I typically would suggest we take a moment to celebrate our victory, I do need to point out that we currently have a gentleman dangling upside down in the well." Gideon jabbed his thumb in Azrael's direction. "Despite his wiry stature, I can assure you he's quite scrappy. If you ladies will help me, we can get him marked and back in control of his senses."

Nose crinkling, Malaria clucked her tongue against the roof of her mouth. "You two hold him and I'll carve the symbol. Mine looks like it was hacked on by a drunken monkey."

My stare lobbed from Malaria to Gideon.

Even with a mask on, the pirate could read me well. "There was a chance she was going to eat your face off. Freeing her was our only option."

"Fine," I grumbled, stomping over to the well. "But I think Charlie was on to something. At least her way, she was quiet."

Pulling the rope hand over hand, Gideon raised Azrael topside. As soon as the soles of his shoes were visible, Malaria and I grabbed ahold of him and heaved him onto the ground.

"Ugh!" Malaria grimaced. "Is that what I looked like? That is *not* flattering."

With a chorus of inhuman grunts, Azrael threw himself wildly from side to side. In the midst of his thrashing, the moonlight reflected off something glittering from the socket of his galaxy-infused eye. "What is *that*? Hold him."

Gideon planted a hand on each of Azrael's shoulders, allowing me to examine the artifact. Two stones—one round and the other teardrop-shaped—polished to gleaming perfection and strung together with gold wiring. "It looks like some sort of primitive jewelry. How the heck did it find its way into his eye socket?"

Malaria shrugged. "People drop things down there all the time, and your boy toy bounced him off a couple of walls on the way up. He's lucky all his teeth are still intact."

"Hey!" Gideon interjected, the perfect bow of his lips sinking into a frown. "He was flailing like a mackerel! It wasn't intentional!"

"Regardless," Malaria talked over him, "it will allow us to get close enough to mark him without getting mesmerized by the cosmic hole in his skull. I say we leave it. Truth be told, it looks better than those tired shrouds he insists on hiding it behind."

Lips pursed, I shook my head. "I never thought I would say these words, but I liked you better as a zombie."

FIVE

"*Masochistic goblin*!" Azrael spat in Malaria's direction, his hand applying pressure to the newly carved mark on his forearm. "You could have at least *pretended* not to enjoy that."

Rising from her crouched position, Malaria flipped her hair over her shoulder. "Why would I waste your time, or mine, attempting to deny something so obvious?"

Face fixed in a deep scowl, Azrael parted his fingers to peek at the artwork carved into his flesh. "You're saying this will block Charlie's influence? You've tested it and are certain?"

Hooking one hand under the concierge's arm, Gideon helped him to his feet. "Aye. I marched right up to her and found she had no pull over me at all. That said, we can't let her know we've discovered this. When you see her controlling others around you, play puppet right along with them."

Lip pressed in a thin white line, Azrael dipped his head in a resolute nod. "Of course. But, can I mark others? Prevent newcomers to the island from being victimized so soon after death?"

Fingers curling around the front hem of my cloak, I pulled it tighter around me to fight off the chill of night. "You need to return to the resort and mark anyone you can, but make sure all of them know to be discreet. We can't risk Charlie learning that we've found a way to block the only real power she has."

"So, what are you and lover boy going to do to bring little sister down, while the rest of us are putting our own safety at risk by secretly slicing into folks?" Malaria folded her bony arms across her chest and lifted her chin defiantly.

Unable to voice the claims about my father out loud, I opted for a more neutral response. "Bones gave me the name of someone he believes may be able to help; a recluse who lives on the outskirts of the island. I'd feel a lot better about leaving to track him down if I wasn't worried Charlie was going to utilize that time finding new and horrifying ways to torture my people."

Chewing on the inside of her cheek, Malaria's eyes narrowed. "What we need is someone to distract her. To get into her head and twist her priorities."

Gideon's spine instantly stiffened. "You can't possibly mean…"

Flicking one wrist in annoyance, Malaria shriveled him with a glare. "Can you think of any other way?"

My wide-eyed stare lobbed from Gideon to Malaria and back again. "Any idea what they're talking about?" I muttered to Azrael.

Ghostly complexion fading to an ashen gray, Azrael ignored my question completely. "Don't you think that will make things monumentally worse? In no way can he be trusted!"

"Not feeling good about whoever this is," I mused, lips parting with a pop.

"He's loyal to whomever has the upper hand. We just have to make sure that's us." Even Malaria didn't seem convinced by her own weak argument. "I mean, if he's still around, he's lived with Tempest and has felt her strength. That may be enough to sway him into our corner while they go in search of help."

Rapidly blinking, I struggled to keep up in the conversation quickly spiraling out of comprehension. "What now? Who lived with Tempest?"

Wetting her lips, Malaria adopted a sugary-sweet tone that was somehow more terrifying than anything they had said thus far. "He's known as The Friendly Houseguest, and last I heard, he lived within the walls of Legba Manor."

I sat down hard on the edge of the Screaming Well. "I'm sorry… *he lives in the walls*? Like, watching me sleep, bathe, or… whatever?"

A playful grin teased at the corners of Gideon's lips. "I'd like to circle back to that *whatever* later."

Keeping his face at an impassive neutral, Azrael hunted for a diplomatic answer. "Don't think of it as a peeping Tom-type situation. It's more comparable to one of those little fishes that ride around on the back of a shark, catching whatever bits of loose food they can. But in this case, he's feeding off the ripples of energy whenever you use your powers."

"So… he's a glorified leech hiding in my walls. Not feeling better about this Houseguest guy."

Kneeling at my side, Gideon took my hand in his. "I'm so sorry. I would have said something if I believed he was still there. I honestly thought he vanished when Legba did, and moved on when the power he fed off for decades was gone."

"I can't say for sure that he hasn't." Malaria shifted her weight from one foot to the other. "But if he *is* still lingering around there, he might be just what we need to distract Charlie. He can whisper in her ear and fill her head with enough doubts to keep her distracted… for a while, at least."

Thumb nervously tracing the edge of the stone beneath my knee, I chewed on the inside of my cheek. "How do we find out if he's still there?"

Fiddling with the jewelry in his eye, Azrael popped it out for a look before situating it back in place. "We talk to the one person more tuned into this island than anyone else."

All four of us chorused one name in unison. "Ember."

SIX

Fingers closing around the doorknob to Hollow's End Apothecary, I hesitated before pulling it open. "She could be under Charlie's influence just like Azrael and Malaria were. We need to be prepared for that possibility. When we get inside, we need to surround her… fast. Move quickly and be cautious, unless she lunges and tries to rip anyone's face off. In which case we tackle her and hold her down long enough for Malaria to mark her."

Malaria's face brightened with a beaming grin. "I'm thrilled that's become my job. I think I would have been a much more pleasant person in life if it was socially acceptable to stab people."

Ignoring her, Gideon placed a hand on my shoulder and gave a gentle squeeze of support. "We've got your back, *mo bhanrion*. Whatever it takes."

"Within reason," Azrael corrected, smoothing the front of his tuxedo coat. "I'm not going to walk into a burning building for her. But perhaps one that's really humid and makes my hair look weird."

"This pep talk has been very reassuring. Thank you," I deadpanned, then yanked open the door.

One step inside, and we were enveloped by the comforting smell of herbs and old parchment. From its perch atop the bookshelf in the corner, Ember's owl flapped his wings to welcome us into the establishment.

Well aware its ruffled feathers served another purpose, I jerked my head in the direction of the apothecary's avian friend. "Assume she already knows we're here, and spread out. We find her... *now*."

"I can assure you there is no need for such urgency." Behind the front counter, Ember gathered sage into bundles that she hung upside down on hooks to dry. "Charlie has no influence over me."

Floorboards creaking under my feet, I ducked under hanging jars as I cautiously approached her. "Are you magically impervious to her, just like you could somehow miraculously communicate with the Rofenod?"

Dressed in a demure, pilgrim-style dress with long cuffed sleeves and a high collar, Ember folded her hands politely on the countertop. "I have already explained about the Rofenod and the blank spots in my memory surrounding that circumstance. As for your sister..." Trailing off, she turned her left hand palm up and shoved back her sleeve to reveal the Hamsa already carved into her skin.

"Man," Malaria tsked, "I was really looking forward to doing that."

Brows knit tightly together, my eyes narrowed. "How did you know to do that?"

Ember's head tilted, the motion causing her blunt bob haircut to bounce against her jawline. "You remember I'm a seer, right? Not too farfetched a notion for me to have a vision of something as important as this symbol."

Taking off my mask, I tucked it under my arm and shook out my hair. "If I ask what else you've seen, am I going to get another cryptic rhyme?"

In a blink, Ember's features fell stone serious. "Unfortunately, I can't even offer that. I've tried to see what's to come, but there are too many alternatives as of yet. I sincerely wish I could be more helpful in that regard."

"So do I." Combing the fingers of my free hand through my hair, I ached for the weight of my crown, missing its presence like a severed limb. "But I do have another favor to ask. The last time I was here, I came in search of a monster. It would seem that's becoming a habit."

Leaning a hip against the counter, Ember folded her arms across her chest. "If you're seeking The Host, they are still at The Home Deadpot. The rest of the vendors cleared out when your sister arrived, choosing to go into hiding like so many of our residents. But, last I heard, they remained there with their television set."

"It's not The Host I'm looking for this time. We need... what's his name?" Chin to my shoulder, I glanced to Gideon, my mind drawing a blank.

Clearing his throat, Gideon uttered his moniker as if it tasted foul on his tongue. "The Friendly Houseguest."

Jaw swinging slack, her wide-eyed stare flicked from the fair-haired pirate to me. "*Why, in Legba's name, would you want to do that*? He can't be trusted for *anything* except to put his own interests before anything and anyone else."

Plucking a jar of cinnamon sticks from a shelf, Malaria unscrewed the cap to smell the contents. "As much fun as it is to have our time wasted by you stating the obvious, we are well aware he'll stab us in the back the first chance he gets. Unfortunately, he's also the only one who can truly distract Charlie. I mean, sure, Azrael can hypnotize people, but he's more of a minute man who can't sustain his talents for much longer than that." Glancing at the former astronaut, she lifted one shoulder in a half-assed shrug. "No offense."

"Some taken," he scoffed.

"So, is he still here?" Resting my mask on the counter, I leaned in, hanging on her every word. "Is there a way we can contact him and ask for help?"

Tapping her shoulder, Ember called the owl to her and paused to scratch the feathers under his beak before answering. "He's here, alright. But mark my words, summoning him will only make things worse."

Running a finger over one of Ember's shelves, Azrael cringed at the dust he found there. "Worse than a curly-haired strumpet who's only been alive a couple of decades bending us to her every whim and desire? That's truly hard to imagine."

"Then you're blinded by ignorance." Ember slapped one palm onto the countertop, the powerful clap it made demanding our attention. "Little by little, my memories of the time Tempest and Charlie spent here as children have been coming back. Some of the darkest recollections from their youth were tarnished by The Houseguest. He lived in the manor walls, content in feeding off ripples of energy from Legba's mighty power. Then, the Legba girls were born. Tempest, you had magic like your father and could have provided The Guest with many meals without issue at all. But Charlie? She was true decadence to him. Her heart was dark and easily corruptible. He whispered to her. Fed into her insecurities and building rage. Prompted her to act out, then gobbled up the hate that emanated off of her when she did. Legba entombed him in the same walls that housed him and made it impossible for him to feed or escape, all in hopes of saving his girls. But it was too late. The evil within Charlie had grown to a dangerous beast that could no longer be ignored. And... well... we know how that tale is currently playing out."

"That's why he's in the wall?" I tapped the tip of one fingernail on my mask, trying to keep up. "Because Legba put him there?"

"Ah! That one *I* can answer." Azrael wagged one finger in the air. "Not all of us need to get all cloudy-eyed to know things. Some simply *listen.* " He shot a pointed look in Ember's direction, then turned his full attention my way. "You see, in life, he was an officer of the law who took great pride in upholding justice. Citizens adored him. Criminals feared him. Those he imprisoned in jail cells loathed him with a fiery passion. One night, there was a riot in a local prison. A dozen or so inmates escaped. A handful of which decided that was the perfect opportunity to get revenge on the dutiful officer. Arming themselves with any weapons they could steal or snag, they headed to his house. While he wasn't home, his lovely wife was. They hurt that poor child in unspeakable ways, yet denied her the mercy of death. They wanted her husband to find her, and spend every day after haunted by how he failed her whenever he looked at her."

Gideon tried to lean an elbow on a shelf, only to knock over a bottle of oil sitting there. "How did that land him in the wall?" Righting the bottle, he used his forearm to wipe away the spill.

Ember tossed Gideon a towel from her desk to clean off his arm and picked up the story. "Something changed in him after that. He vowed never to let anything happen to her again. Quit his job. Never left her side. What started as an act of compassion morphed into obsession. He stalked her every move. Followed her everywhere she went. Constantly kept a watchful eye on her."

"I'm sure you can imagine how easy it would be to take such a thing too far," Azrael interjected.

"And he did." Ember nodded in agreement. "Feeling stifled from her own healing because of his demanding needs, his wife kicked him out. The troubled officer didn't take that rejection well. He became crazed. Manic. One night he broke into the home they once shared, demanding she take him back. It escalated to a violent confrontation."

Azrael's head tilted with compassion, the jewel in his eye socket glimmered in the glow from Ember's lanterns strung overhead. "In the process of fending off his crushing affections, his wife thought she had killed him. Acting out of panic, she walled his body up behind a layer of bricks in their home. Only… he wasn't dead. He came to and went right back to watching over her every day. He should have died quickly without food or water, but rumor has it, madness kept him alive, nourishing him simply by being near her. Which is why he continued to feed off the energies of others even after death."

"And it's because of that same insatiable hunger that I highly recommend you keep that far-from-friendly Houseguest right where he is." Even as she spoke, Ember pulled a quill and inkwell from a shelf beneath the counter. A dip of the tip and her hand began moving over a sheet of parchment in quick strokes. "He will take our horrible situation and make it far more… messy. That said, you are the one true Queen and are often forced to make impossible decisions in the face of unfathomable odds." Setting her quill aside, she rounded the counter to grab a cloudy white crystal from a shelf. Wrapping the parchment around it, she placed it in my hand. "It is for that reason alone that I am entrusting you with this. Hold the crystal. Utter the words. Call out her name. That is all you need, and that's also where my help in this matter ends. I want no part in calling forth The Houseguest, and if you're truly concerned with the well-being of Carnage Crossing… neither should you."

SEVEN

"You have to realize this is insane." Gideon trailed me across the back lawn of Legba Manor, matching my speed in hopes of deterring me. "Without The Houseguest to distract your sister, we are *literally* walking into the viper's pit. And the fact that you sent Malaria and Azrael away when numbers could work in our favor? If you had a pulse, I'd think you had a death wish."

Tripping over a cobblestone paver at the edge of the patio, I steadied my footing and strode on towards the middle set of French doors. "I know it might not seem like it, but this is me reverting to our original plan. We're going to find the Rofenod. But first, there's something I have to get." Biting my lower lip, I tried the back door. Having recently been replaced, it didn't creak open like the others but silently welcomed us inside with a rush of air. "In and out, quick and quiet. That's why I sent the other two away; it betters the odds we won't draw attention to ourselves."

Gideon's head moved on a swivel, searching for incoming threats. "And what is it we're looking for?"

Moving on whispered steps, I ventured inside the empty ballroom. "My father's journal. Charlie got her hands on our mother's and found a way to boot stomp her way through the Veil. I have no desire to see what she's capable of if she gets ahold of Legba's."

Easing the door shut behind us, Gideon stayed right by my side as we tiptoed through the darkness. "Where's the last place you saw it?"

Swallowing hard, I said a silent prayer of thanks that my features were hidden behind the faux skull. I could keep my tone neutral, but my face would have told the true story of my unease. "Where I left it. Under the pillow… in my bedroom."

Gideon stopped cold. His hand encircled my wrist as he tugged me back to face him. "Is there any chance at all your sister has picked a *different* room to claim as her own?"

"I mean, it's a big manor. Maybe she wanted a smaller bedroom, without a private bathroom or magnificent view of the entire town. Because… who would want those things, right?"

Even in the dim lighting, I could see Gideon's mouth twisted into a frown. "If you think that sounded at all convincing, I have news for you." Chin falling to his chest, he rubbed a hand over the back of his neck. "You have to see this for the unnecessary risk it is. She—"

"*Shhhhh.*" Wisps of green and purple rippled down my arms, black rot tipping each of my fingers. "We aren't alone."

Side by side we crept, both of us gripping a blade tight.

We found him in the hall of the otherwise silent estate.

Mel.

Or, what was left of his shattered existence.

He stood stone still, his shoulders slumped and stare vacant, waiting for direction from the master pulling his strings.

Sniffing back the black-tinged tears that welled in my eyes, I jerked my head towards his arm. "We can't leave him here like this. Hold him still; I'll mark him."

Gideon didn't argue, but forced up Mel's sleeve and offered me his forearm. As I worked, carving out each line, he went over our plan of escape. "We take back halls from here, and avoid high-traffic areas. The instant you get your hands on the journal, we clear out through the nearest door or window we can find. No further detours."

"No further detours," Mel parroted, his stare blinking into focus as I finished the Hamsa design. "Except to free Lugosi. She keeps him upstairs. I don't know what she does to him, but..." chin trembling, his voice quaked with emotion, "I can hear his screams."

Through the mesh lining of my mask, Gideon and I locked stares. Both of us knowing, good or bad, our plans had just changed.

"We'll find him, I promise." Carefully as I could, I eased his sleeve back down over the mark. "Azrael is back at the resort. Why don't you head over there, and—"

"No!" Adamantly, he shook his head. "I'm not leaving without Lugosi. If you're going to find him, I'm going with you."

While his gaze burned into me, Gideon clapped a hand on Mel's shoulder. "Aye, I respect that. I wouldn't be able to leave my love behind either. We have to move quickly. Think you can keep up?"

Physically shaking off the fear and sorrow eating at him, Mel gave a resolute nod. "For Lugosi, I will."

Our trio moved like shadows up the narrow back staircase and through the second-floor hall. Slinking down the corridor, we peeked into each room we came across in search of Lugosi or the journal. Urgency built each time we came up empty-handed. With only my bed chambers left, a sense of dread throbbed around us like a beating pulse.

The door hung open like the gaping jaws of a crocodile ready to deliver unspeakable pain. One step inside, and I had to clap a hand over my mouth to squelch a scream.

"Mel, don't look," I managed as he skidded to a stop behind me.

But it was too late.

With a choked gasp, his legs buckled and the floor rose to meet him.

EIGHT

Lugosi's hands were bound over his head, the rope holding him strung to the wooden beam that ran the length of the ceiling. His face was swollen and bruised, his lower lip split and dripping black blood. Dressed in a tuxedo shirt that was open to the naval, the vest and matching slacks he wore were still pinned in place. As if a tailor had popped in for a fitting in the middle of him being mercilessly tortured.

Hearing our collective gasps, he raised his head and managed a lopsided grin on painfully puffy features. "Believe it or not, this isn't what it looks like."

Swallowing hard, I fought off the black rage creeping into the edges of my vision. "Cut him down," I rasped.

While Gideon crossed the room in three wide strides to do just that, I hooked an arm under Mel's pits and let him lean on me as we followed behind.

"Not what it looks like?" Gideon grumbled, breaking the first tie with one easy swipe of his blade. "So the youngest child of Legba didn't use you as a punching bag? Or stand back and watch while someone else did?"

One arm free, Lugosi sagged with exhaustion, making it necessary for Gideon to prop up his slack form to cut the second tie.

"Oddly enough, that wasn't the case. *This* is from a beating from days gone but never forgotten." Lugosi winced in pain as Gideon eased him down onto my bed.

"Your Witching Hour," I guessed, knowing all too well the violent nature of his death.

Eyes narrowed and blinking hard to focus, Lugosi leaned in to see better. "Good guess. I think they knocked something loose this time, too. Because Tempest's head looks *really* swollen… and bony."

"Lugosi?" Shoving past me, Mel dove to his fiancé's side, taking a knee on the floor in front of him. "Are you okay?"

Lugosi placed the palm of his thumbless hand on Mel's cheek. "I am, now that you're by my side. And, really, this," he gestured to his mangled face with his free hand, "isn't nearly as bad as it looks. My Witching Hour struck in the middle of my tuxedo fitting. Charlie didn't quite know what to make of it…"

"So, she tied you to the rafters," I marveled in disgust. "I think I missed that lesson in first aid during nursing school."

"I tried yelling our safe word," Lugosi chuckled, then winced from what appeared to be a broken rib. "Somehow, I think screaming *Meatloaf* just added to her thinking that I was having some sort of episode."

"None of that matters now." Mel shook his head, one flaxen lock of hair falling across his forehead. 'We're getting you out of here."

Sad resignation clouded Lugosi's handsome features. Catching Mel's hand, he brought it to his lips and kissed the delicate skin between his knuckles. "I can't leave with you. Not if we want to give Tempest a chance to stop Charlie. She's put the crown on. Sat on the throne. It doesn't matter. Those artifacts don't grant her the Legba power. She's convinced marrying me will—mostly because I'm a hell of a salesman who had her buying into all that pomp before all this mess began."

Behind my mask, I rolled my eyes; not in annoyance, but relief that his sense of self-adoration was still thriving. "Weird flex for a guy who was tied to the ceiling when we walked in, but go on."

"My point, puffy-headed Tempest," he teased, letting his head lob in my direction, "is if I vanish and deny her the opportunity to try out this theory she's so invested in, she will burn this whole island down hunting for me."

"If you're staying, I'm staying." Mel's chin jutted out with his bold proclamation.

"No! You're going to go and help Tempest any way you can."

Catching hold of his hand, Mel held it in a white-knuckled grip of unwavering dedication. "Forever in death. Those were the words we said to one another when we decided to get married. I don't care if we haven't said our vows yet. I will stand by your side forever in death because you are my heart. My happiness. And my reason for everything."

As the two men shared their tender moment, I reached under my pillow and found Legba's journal right where I left it. Folding it in half, I tucked it under my cloak in the back of my belt, only to knock the crystal and spell Ember gave me out of that same hiding spot.

Bouncing across the wooden floorboards, the milky white stone bumped into the side of Lugosi's bare foot. "What is this?" As he posed the question, he picked up the stone and the parchment around it fell open in his hand.

"*That* is nothing." Trying to diminish its importance, I took it back and tossed it on the bed.

Lugosi's brows disappeared into his hairline, the marks from his Witching Hour quickly fading. "Really? Because it looks like the spell to call forth The Friendly Houseguest." Noticing how I bristled, he cocked his head and offered me a tight-lipped grin. "No need to look shocked. You might be Queen, but my fine ass has been swishing around these parts *a lot* longer than yours."

Dragging my tongue over my lower lip, I huffed a humorless laugh. "Fair enough. Still, from what I've heard of this Guest guy, he's anything *but* friendly. Therefore I would like to keep the pin in that particular grenade. Especially since we have another, far more potent weapon in our arsenal."

"What exactly is going on in here?" a familiar voice interrupted.

I didn't have to look her way to know who she was. I could hear the deafening pulse of her beating heart pounding into my temples like railroad spikes.

The only living one found in Carnage Crossing.

Charlie.

Head slowly turning in her direction, I felt the pull of my ghoulish side taking over. My skin paled, black veins tracking beneath my flesh. Hidden beneath my mask, I made no attempt to shake off those attributes of rot. Not when they so perfectly represented the hollow ache I felt when I looked at her. The Charlie I knew was dead, exorcised from existence to bring forth the monster before me.

Hands on her hips, Charlie sashayed into the room with her freshly glossed lips pursed. The dress she wore was one Malaria designed for me. Unlike her, I could never bring myself to wear it because of the skanky way the sparkly silver fabric plunged to my pelvis.

"Because it looks to me like you're trying to steal my groom." Sauntering straight up to Mel, she adjusted the collar of his shirt, allowing the points of her fingernails to brush against his neck. "Which, I have to say, would surprise me. Not because I'm in any way oblivious to your feelings for my betrothed. I see you mooning over him like a lovesick puppy. I just didn't think you had it in you."

"He isn't yours." Any traces of Mel's normal timidness vanished, replaced by pure venom. "And I'm not leaving here without—"

"*Giving you the gift he brought for you!*" Lugosi cut in.

I was enraged being that close to my sister. Craved violent chaos, just sharing the same space as her. But the instant those words left Lugosi's lips, all my emotions were replaced by icy dread.

"What are you doing?" I disguised my voice with a throaty growl.

"Aw, come on! Don't be shy. How could any queen be cross, knowing some of her subjects gathered to honor her with a special tribute?" Before I could move to stop him, Lugosi spun on his heel and snatched the quartz crystal and spell off the mattress.

Jaw locked tight, Gideon's words came through clenched teeth. "Are you sure about this, Lugosi? We haven't had time to… wrap her gift. Or decide the perfect time to give it to her."

"No time like the present!" Lugosi bubbled in mock enthusiasm and stabbed both items in Charlie's direction.

Upturned nose crinkling, Charlie curled one lock of hair around her finger as she peered down at his offering. "What is this? A jewelry-making kit?"

Braving a step closer, Lugosi blinked up at her with what appeared to be genuine sincerity… even to me. "This will grant you your deepest desires. All your fantasies will come to life if you hold the stone and utter the words."

Mel looked from Lugosi to me, trying to piece together what was happening. The only clarification I could offer was a slight shake of my head.

Picking up on my not-so-subtle warning, Mel hid a cough behind his hand. "Uh, Lugosi? Don't things like this usually come at some sort of cost? You should let her know about that upfront."

"There's no cost for loyalty, I assure you." Where Charlie had her doll hidden in that revealing dress, I'd rather not think about. But with a sleight of hand and roll of her wrist, it appeared gripped tightly in her fist. "Unless it's to my sister, in which case the penalty will be quite severe."

"And devotion to the one, *true* Queen is *exactly* my intention." The offering outstretched before him, Lugosi dipped in a half-curtsy. Head bowed, he tossed a hidden glance and a wink in my direction. "Hold the stone and read the words aloud, and a being will be summoned that will help you achieve even your loftiest goals."

I tried to bump his arm and knock the crystal from his hand.

My effort came too late.

Tucking her doll under her arm, Charlie cradled her gift in her hands while a look of ravenous hunger dilated her pupils. Her gaze moved from side to side, reading the words on the parchment as if anticipating a trap. When nothing written there triggered warning alarms in her mind, she wet her lips and began.

"Creature trapped within our walls,
we beseech you now to hear our call.
Entombed by she unworthy of your love,
come to us now and rise above.
Join us from your place of rest.
We call forth... The Friendly Houseguest."

The quartz crystal pulsed with light from within, each flash growing in intensity and building to a blinding glow.

Charlie's eyes widened to goose eggs, that strobing white light reflecting in the depths of her stare as she continued.

"Channel your passion, redirect its aim.
Find a welcome recipient when I gift you their name."

Don't get me wrong, my sister was public enemy number one. That said, facing off with her right there in Legba manor seemed the preferable alternative to allowing a creature to come forward that would take her from menacing psychopath to full-fledged monster on a rampage.

With that in mind, I stepped forward and made no attempts to mask my voice. "Charlie, please. Drop the stone."

See my fatal mistake there?

Because I didn't at the time.

The first word out of my mouth... gifted The Guest her name.

If she heard me, she didn't let on. Her attention locked on whatever was playing out for her eyes only. What it was, I couldn't say, but a dreamy look washed over her features. Breath catching in her throat, Charlie let one hand flutter to her chest as she batted her lashes at the wall behind her. "You... look like Chris Evans on the cover of a romance novel. All Vaselined up with your hair blowing in the breeze."

The rest of us... did not get that version.

He emerged from the wall in a gruesome soundtrack of squishy slurps and bone-chilling crunches. Attention locked on Charlie, he curled and hovered around her with a passion that could only be described as manic. "My Queen, my beauty. Tell me your heart's desire and I will give all of myself to make it so."

Reaching under my mask, I covered my mouth with my hand out of fear that what little contents there were in my stomach were about to revolt. "Uh, do we know by chance if The Houseguest's wife took an ax to his gut before sealing him up in the wall?"

Complexion morphing from gray to green, Gideon grimaced. "That would explain the entrails spilling from his midsection in thick, dripping ropes."

Clamping his lips around a giggle/whimper, Mel waved one finger in the direction of the newcomer. "What's with the black ooze seeping between his teeth?"

Before we could form any guesses, Charlie peered up at him with a lustful gaze, her breasts heaving beneath the thin fabric of her gown. The Guest rewarded her attentions by taking her in his grime-covered arms and crushing her mouth to his. Sludge squished between their mashed faces, dripping from their chins in heavy splats.

So many more important matters at hand, yet I was temporarily stuck on the train wreck before me. "This whole island was rotting just a few days ago, but *that* is without a doubt the grossest thing I have ever seen."

Lugosi tried to loop his thumbs in the front pockets of his slacks, only to get the awkward reminder he was now down a digit. Still, he tried not to let that tarnish his momentary victory. "We needed her distracted so all of you could get out of here. Now, she's distracted. You're welcome."

The Houseguest kissed his way around to the back of Charlie's neck, his lower intestine slapping between them with the motion.

"Whatever you want. Anything you long for. My greatest thrill will be catering to your every... *desire.*" The way he uttered that last word was damned near pornographic.

"Yes, thank you for... *this.*" There was no way those images were ever leaving my brain. I was also convinced my face would henceforth be stuck in a cringe. "That said, the last time these two were together, he coerced her into all sorts of unspeakable acts. So, kudos on throwing gasoline on the fire."

Lugosi's arms fell slack at his sides. "Well, how was I supposed to know *that*?"

Eyebrows rocketing to his hairline, Mel's entire upper body swiveled his way. "All of us were trying to warn you! Not even with subtle clues, but with blatant alarm sirens you willfully chose to ignore!"

Hands raised to halt further discussion, Lugosi shrugged off the entire matter. "Regardless, she's distracted. So you need to go, *now.*"

"What about you two?" Gideon rumbled, still ready to fight his way out of the room if need be.

Lacing his fingers with Lugosi's, Mel formed a united front with his love. "I'll mark him. We'll look out for each other. You two go, don't worry about us. Just do whatever it takes to save Carnage Crossing."

I wanted to argue further, even as Gideon grabbed hold of my upper arm and led me to the open window. But it was the voice in my head that squashed any protest I may have had.

In the middle of mashing his tongue down my sister's throat, The Houseguest locked stares with me across the room. His voice echoed off the walls of my mind in an ominous hiss not to be ignored. "*She's not the only one with power here, girl. I can feel it wafting off you in heady waves. One way or another, I will tap into the true darkness of this island... and make it mine.*"

NINE

In the two days that followed, Gideon and I combed the outskirts of the island in search of the Rofenod. Our travels took us from the rocky shoreline where he anchored the Marie Ann, to the steep incline of the north bank where Mel's treehouse was perched and everything in between. No trace of the creature was anywhere to be found.

I'd like to say I was at least enjoying the time alone with my sexy pirate, but that would imply that I had my full senses about me. Which I did not. My mind was haunted by the voice of The Houseguest; whispering my failures, tempting me to act.

Standing atop the Worm's Wart Dam, I peered out at the ominous black fissures stretching across the emerald and amethyst swirls of the Veil and found myself too exhausted to block out his taunting.

"*She chased you from your home. Made slaves of your people. Yet here you are, hunting for someone else to be the salvation to you all.* You *are the savior they need.* You *are that hero.*"

Tipping my face to the winds lashing through the valley, I prayed they would cleanse my mind of his tainted dark whisperings.

"Your sister's heart still beats and she's committed horribly atrocious acts. Kill her. Snuff out her life, knowing her soul is far too rotten to ever end up here. Think of how easy it would be. You could take your time. Really make it hurt..."

"Tempest?" Gideon's voice was cool, soothing aloe on a scorched burn, offering me a moment of relief from what had become a near-constant ache. "Your hands, love... are you okay?"

I couldn't say I was surprised to glance down and see them black with rot. Thanks to the mind games of The Guest, my ghoulish side had started making surprise cameos whether I liked it or not. Yet another reason this trip hadn't been a romantic interlude for Gideon and me... It was hard to get your sexy on when you suddenly looked like roadkill.

"I'm fine." Unsure if I could shake off my black-tipped fingers, I straightened my arms at my sides and let the sleeves of the shirt I borrowed from him fall and hide my hands.

"The voice is back?" His question wasn't meant to pry but voiced genuine concern.

Lips pressed in a thin line, all I could manage was a weak nod.

Gideon said nothing, only offering me his hand. Only when I placed my palm in his did he lace his fingers with mine and lead me off the dam towards the cave in the cliffs where we made our makeshift camp for the night.

No sooner did our shoes sink in the dirt, the arch of the dam behind us, than Gideon pulled up short. Chest puffed, his gaze searched the tree line for signs of movement.

"Don't tell me you're hearing voices, too," I scoffed, one brow hitched in half-hearted interest. "Not sure how much help we'll be to Carnage Crossing if we both go batshit crazy."

Letting go of my hand, Gideon pulled the dagger from the sheath on his hip. "We aren't alone."

Squeezing my eyes shut, I tried to wrangle up some iota of concern. A difficult task when my own thoughts were constantly being invaded. The best I could offer was, "Friend or foe?"

"Neither, and yet… both," Gideon snorted in the same instant Malaria stepped out from behind a rapidly growing white ash tree.

All that she had seen, so many morsels of information about the town that she held, yet her immediate reaction was to crinkle her nose at the black pants I'd partnered with Gideon's flowy linen shirt. "Seriously, have I taught you nothing? You couldn't at least tie a belt around your waist so you look less boxy?"

Head falling to the side, I peered at her through narrowed eyes. "Malaria. Why are you here?"

"If I had to point my finger on it? The final straw that chased me out of town was probably your sister's horrible fashion sense. I mean, *you're* a mess, but at least you take direction well." Once more, she scanned my ensemble. "For the most part. But that sister of yours? She has all the curves of a yardstick, yet insists I make a mermaid-style wedding dress for her. You have to have *an ass* to pull that off! *Everyone knows that*!"

"Malaria," Gideon's gruff tone guided her back to the subject at hand. "In no way do either of us believe that's what chased you out here."

Rolling her eyes, the fashion designer folded her arms over her chest. "Fine, if you must know, I came looking for you because Charlie has crippled the entire town. All the businesses have shut down and all the residents are in hiding. They come out when called on to do something for the upcoming nuptials, then go back in hiding from Charlie's wrath. And, thanks to The Friendly Houseguest, her methods have become far more vindictive. He whispers that her rule is pure artistry and coerces her to be her very worst, and all of us suffer because of it."

Easing my weary bones down on a boulder, I rested my elbows on my knees. "How so?"

Cocking one hip, Malaria stabbed a fist onto it. "Would you like examples of the physical or emotional torture?"

If there was a good answer to that question, I didn't know it. Lips parting with a pop, the word came out as more of a question than a declaration. "Uh… emotional?"

"Oh, wonderful," Malaria sneered. "Try this one for size. Charlie is making Mel be a part of the planning process because she knows how much it hurts him. To get him to be an active participant, she threatened to flog Lugosi unless Mel admitted what heartfelt elements he would want in *his* wedding. Not wanting to see his lover in more pain than necessary, Mel confessed that his grandmother was from the Ukraine… or someplace like that. Every Christmas she told the story of the Christmas Spider. According to him—and keep in mind I was only half-listening—a rogue pinecone caused an evergreen to grow in the hut of a poor widow who couldn't feed her kids. The tree grew and grew, which gave them a beautiful Christmas tree, but is pretty much fucking pointless if you're starving. Without the money to decorate it, the whole family cried themselves to sleep that Christmas Eve. While they slept, a spider spun a bunch of webs on the tree, which somehow—and this sounds like complete horseshit to me—turned into silver and gold in the morning light. The family never had to worry about money again and decorated their tree with spiderwebs every Christmas after that. Charlie heard that story and decided her wedding to Lugosi would be filled with Christmas bulbs and spiderwebs… for no other reason than to turn the knife deeper in Mel's heart."

With the back of my fist to my lips, I wanted to be disgusted over the kind of mind that would purposely hurt another like that. However, I couldn't dig into that level of depravity when I knew it wasn't the end. "And the physical?"

Malaria paused for a beat, her tongue dragging over her bottom lip. "She and The Houseguest decided to experiment with the fortitude of a dead skeleton. They took Bones apart, piece by piece, and rearranged him into a morbid candelabra. The only thing that silenced his screams was Charlie wiring his jaws shut. Now, he hangs over her bed holding six black candles. Deep in the black pits of his eye sockets, you can still see the red light of life flickering from within."

Silence was the only response to such horror.

There were no excuses.

No explanations that could make these horrific events okay.

"Bones." My voice betrayed me by quivering at the mention of his name. "He told me to find the Rofenod. He claims that it was my father who first discovered the protective power of the Hamsa hand. Fearing for the safety of the island, he marked himself with it. Then… he was exorcised. The mark prevented his soul from being vanquished. Instead, it mutated him… into the Rofenod."

For a beat, Malaria was quiet, as if she was hunting for the right words. "How could Bones possibly know that?"

"You remember the Royal Vizier Bram? Well, that was Bones before he banished himself from town over how he felt he failed the royal family." Rubbing my hands up and down my arms, I tried to fight off the chill skittering down my spine. "He was there when all of this went down, and the memories of me and Charlie being here were wiped from the minds of every resident… but him. We've searched everywhere for the creature, and he seems to have vanished. I don't know what else to do. Everything I built and restored, my sister has wiped away with a flick of her wrist, like it never mattered at all."

Malaria's face crinkled in disgust. "Okay, I'm going to need the pity party for one to come to a quick halt because it's making me want to die all over again. You broke into the manor for your father's journal. Where is it now?"

Sidestepping, Gideon nodded toward the cave. "In there with the rest of our limited supplies. We've read it from cover to cover, time and again. While the story found in those pages is fascinating, none of it has helped us find the beast, or told us what to do when we do."

Flipping her hair, Malaria shoved past him and strode toward the mouth of the cave with determined strides. "If you're both quite done perfecting your act of being completely inept, how about we find a way to figure this out? Make a fire, pirate. We've got a long night ahead of us."

TEN

Leaning my back against Gideon's chest, I watched the dancing flames of the fire he built. "I think she fell asleep reading." I nodded in the direction of Malaria's slumped frame. Lying on her side with her back to us, one arm was curled under her head like a bony pillow. The other hand, which had been turning the pages of my father's journal, had stilled in its task. "I don't think she had any more luck than we did."

"Not to say that the words he wrote weren't lovely," Gideon murmured against my hair. "His love for your mother was undeniable. He would have given her the world, if he could."

Turning my head, I peered up at him with sleepy eyes. "He tried. He built the town and the manor to make her happy. The fact that all of it was basically poison to her was the true tragedy."

Curling his knuckle under my chin, he tipped my face up to his. "That depends on how you look at it. From where I'm sitting, their romance created the most beautiful sight a bloke could ever behold."

After treating myself to the sweet taste of his lips, I snuggled back into his embrace. "Other than their tragic end, I do envy them in some weird way."

"How so?"

Gaze shifting to the mouth of the cave, I watched the lights of the Veil shimmer off the Oblivion Sea. "They had time. Time to enjoy all the quirky wonderfulness Carnage Crossing has to offer. Time to explore and revel in what they meant to each other. *That* is a luxury we haven't had. We've spent our nights together sleeping with one eye open, ready to fight or flee at a moment's notice. I knew when I married a sexy stranger on the deck of his ship nothing about our relationship would be traditional. Still, a bit of normalcy mixed into the chaos would be a welcome change of pace."

Rubbing his hands up and down my arms, he chased away the chill of the night. "And what would that look like, *mo bhanrion?*"

"For starters," I slapped one hand against the rocky cave floor acting as our bed. "It would involve *furniture*."

Gideon gasped in mock shock. "Stop it!"

"Oh, I know. I have lofty dreams of a pillowtop mattress and Sparrow bringing us some of that glorious, spiced wine she hides somewhere at Legba Manor."

Gideon stiffened behind me… which was saying a lot, considering he was already a corpse. "Tempest… are you implying you'd like us to live together?"

My mouth opened and shut. Unfortunately, I seemed to have lost the ability to form actual words. "Uh… wha… I…" Swallowing hard, I tried again. "That would be crazy, right? I mean, you're a pirate. I'm sure it goes against your seafaring nature not to call the water home. Although, you drowned, so that had to tarnish the allure a bit. Wow. I'm saying a lot of words. And really, all of them are unnecessary, considering this is the worst possible time for us to be having this conversation. I mean, the world is falling apart around us. We don't know if there will be a next week, next month, or next year. Talking about any kind of future at all at this point might as well be fantastical fiction full of flying cars and rainbow farting unicorns."

Ocean blue eyes piercing into me, he gently pressed the matter. "Tempest, is that what you want?"

Before I had the chance to respond, Malaria bolted upright. "*Jewelry*!"

To say I was happy for the interruption would be a vast understatement. "Oh, hey, look! Malaria is up! I can't say I'm surprised that's the first word out of her mouth when she wakes up. The woman has no internal monologue."

Gideon hitched one brow, his almost-smile hinting this matter was far from dropped.

Meanwhile, Malaria scrambled to grab my father's journal and search the pages for whatever hidden nugget prompted her outburst. "It's something your father described in *way* too much detail—I mean really, sum it up, big guy. You fell in love; you didn't invent it."

"Circle back to your point, Malaria," I encouraged, rolling one index finger over the other.

Pulling the parchment pages onto her lap, Malaria pointed to the words scrawled there. "I didn't put it together at first. It seemed like yet another insignificant passage from a man who apparently wanted to remember every minute element of every little thing in excruciating detail. Yet, in one of the entries leading up to Legba's wedding to Belladonna," her gaze flicked from the journal to me, "your mother."

I rolled my eyes. "Yes, I'm familiar with who she is. But thanks for clarifying."

"Anyway, Legba wrote that he wanted their special day to be everything Belladonna dreamed of. To make that happen, he made note of every comment she made in passing about things from the land of the living she wished could be a part of their nuptials." Pausing for a minute, Malaria clucked her tongue against the roof of her mouth. "Listen, I knew your dad was hot. But to learn he was also insanely romantic, *plus* sensitive to her needs and emotions? I've never high-fived another person in the entire length of my existence. But if your mother was here now? High-five. Low-five. On the side. Round the back. A whole celebration of her landing that man."

My entire face folded into a cringe. "We're talking about my parents. Don't make this weird."

Malaria shrugged. "Your dad was a snack. Deal with it."

"And now it's weird."

Dismissing the ick factor, Malaria pushed on. "The one thing Belladonna circled back to time and again involved her grandmother."

"Not surprising. Great Grandma Tilly raised her. In my mother's eyes, G.G. Tilly—as Charlie and I called her—hung the moon. She passed away before my parents were married, but I have no doubt that my mother would have wanted to feel her presence in some way on that day."

"According to this, your grandmother had a pair of candlesticks she only put out for special occasions. They were..." Malaria followed along with her finger as she read. "Intricately crafted from sterling silver and dripping with teardrop pearls."

Chin falling to my chest, I huffed a laugh. "That had to be Legba's interpretation of my mother's words. My mother had many wonderful attributes, but that level of eloquence wasn't one of them."

"Yeah, no one born after, like, nineteen-fifteen talks like that. Legba writes that he wanted to find a way to replicate those candlesticks and surprise your mother with them on their wedding day." Leaning closer to the fire, Malaria squinted to decipher my father's handwriting. "The actual candlesticks weren't hard to come by, though he had to have them forged out of iron instead of silver. The pearls, on the other hand, couldn't be found here."

Chin resting on my shoulder, Gideon seconded that with a nod. "Makes sense. Pearls are made in oysters. Being a living organism, they don't exist here."

"What did he use instead?"

"He didn't want to disappoint her.. at least I think that's what it says." Malaria shook her head, then tucked a rogue lock of hair behind her ear. "Ugh, are that many swoops and swirls really necessary in cursive writing? It shouldn't take a professional linguist to decipher your attempt at elegance! Long story short, he found some pretty rocks, polished them up, and strung them together to resemble those teardrop pearls."

"His lady wanted pearls, he made them happen. Quite commendable, if you ask me." Gideon punctuated the statement by dotting a kiss to the nape of my neck.

Pressing my palm to Gideon's cheek, I playfully scratched the scruff at his jawline. "While it's a cute story, I'm not sure how it helps us."

Clapping the journal shut, Malaria hugged it to her chest. "Because… we've seen the stones from one of those candlesticks before."

Gideon and I exchanged matching masks of confusion before chorusing, "We have?"

The fashion designer couldn't have fought off her victorious smirk if she tried. "Azrael had it wedged in his eye socket when we pulled him up from the Screaming Well."

For a moment I couldn't speak… couldn't wrap my mind around how that could be true. "How can you possibly know it's the same jewel?"

Rolling her eyes, Malaria's shoulders sank in aggravation. "I might not know how the middle class survives on fast food while wearing polyblend clothing, but I *know* jewels. What your dad described is *exactly* what we saw."

"That makes how it ended up in his skull all the more confusing," I grumbled, combing my fingers through my tangled tresses.

"Think about it!" She threw her hands in the air, palms up. "Someone drops through your ceiling with a weirdly hypnotic eye on full display. Gut reaction? You grab the first thing handy to jab in there. In this case, a prettied-up stone that just happens to be eyeball-sized. Why else would artifacts belonging to our beloved king be in the bottom of a well?"

Chewing on the inside of my cheek, I carefully arranged the pieces of the puzzle. "We've looked from one end of this island to the other in search of the Rofenod with no luck. It makes sense it would be beneath us."

Lips pursed, Malaria tapped at her chin with one fingernail. "Quick question; if that *thing* really is Legba—and he *is* hiding down there—what makes you think you can get through to him before he rips your arms off and beats you with them?"

Pushing off the ground, I stood up and paced a slow circle around our campfire. "I have no idea. Not a clue. As of this moment, my plan consists of hoping for the best while preparing for the worst."

Slapping her hands on her knees, Malaria rose to her feet. "Best case scenario? We stop your fashion impaired sister. Worst case? I get to watch you get pummeled by a monster. Either way, I'm in."

ELEVEN

Carnage Crossing had become the ghost town its name implied. The torch lamps that lined the cobblestone streets had been snuffed out. Every storefront was dark, with no signs of movement from within. The eastward winds blew in a heavy fog that rolled across the ground in an ominous warning.

Gideon clutched his dagger in a white-knuckled fist, his gaze on a swivel for threats—dead or alive—lurking in the shadows. "Where is everyone?"

Nostrils flaring, Malaria flipped her hair away from the burned half of her face. "Hiding."

"Hear that?" The Houseguest's voice hissed through my mind, playing off my building doubts. *"Your people have locked themselves away out of fear of your sister, and here you are choosing her life over theirs by not confronting her. Because of Charlie, your throat was cut and you died in a pool of crimson gore. Blood for blood... it's only right."*

My hand shot out at a shadow moving in front of me, expecting to pass right through it and dissipate the wispy mirage. Instead, my fingers curled around the throat of a petite figure hidden beneath a sapphire cloak. "Your Majesty," Ember croaked, quickly pushing off her hood.

With relief and guilt jockeying for position as my primary emotion, I released the apothecary wizard and kept a hand out to steady her. "Ember, I'm so sorry. I'm—"

"On edge," she finished for me with a maternal smile. "And for good reason. That said, I saw something that may be of some help." Stare drifting to the Screaming Well, her eyes morphed to milky white in a blink. "I had a vision, but not of you. A creature from below whose pain is true. When others release their anguish in a desperate wail, he joins the chorus and shrieks to the Veil."

Chin falling to my chest, I reached under my mask to pinch the bridge of my nose between my thumb and index finger. "Of course it comes in rhyme form. Because why wouldn't it?"

Blinking off her seer attributes, Ember fluffed out her cloak and took a seat on the edge of the well. "This one I can explain, with a simple demonstration." Eyes closed, she channeled every ounce of anguish within her and poured an ear-piercing scream to the depths of the well. Instead of letting her scream fade out, as people normally do, she cut it off abruptly. Then, holding up one finger, she mouthed the word, "*Listen.*"

At first, the shriek of response sounded like an echo, one easily dismissed. Until… it carried on two beats longer than Ember's had, the tone deeper in octave. If my heart still beat, it would have been pounding against my ribs. As it was, icy talons of warning cut into me, slicing fear to the marrow of my bones. "He's down there? Malaria was right?"

The fashion designer jerked, one hand fluttering to her chest in a pantomimed flirt. "Say it again louder, and I might just fall in love."

Ignoring Malaria—as we all should—Ember reached under her cloak for a burlap purse drawn tight with a string. Untying it, she dipped two fingers in and pulled them out covered in ash. Bringing them to my forehead she traced a design. "A pentagram of sage to ward off the darkness. Only fear can blind you from the truth. Allow yourself to see him, *truly see him*, and call out his name. That is the only way you can pierce through the ward… at least for a short while."

Despite swallowing hard, even I heard the uneasy quiver in my voice. "Don't be afraid as I'm dropped into a hole occupied by a monster with bone-crushing teeth. That seems easier said than done."

Edging up beside me, Gideon's flask appeared in his hand, seemingly out of nowhere. Unscrewing the cap, he offered me a swig. "Let me go with you, *mo bhanrion*. There is no reason you have to do this alone."

His homemade rum was scorching its way down my gullet when Ember interjected with yet another grim warning. "I'm afraid it can only be her. She's his daughter. His blood. Any more than that and he may think he's under attack. Were that to happen, it would ruin any chance we have to get through to him."

I tipped the flask up once more for good measure before handing it back to my pirate beau. "Show of hands, who wants to lower me to my doom?"

Instantly, Malaria's hand shot in the air.

Ember cringed. "There is *one* more thing."

Plucking off my mask, I handed it to Gideon and shook out my hair. "Of course there is."

Rising to her feet, Ember's cloak fell in waves to her ankles. "I have to take Malaria with me back to the manor."

"I'm totally okay with leaving, but if anyone asks, let's at least say I put up a little bit of a fight." Sidestepping further from the well, Malaria jerked her head for Ember to follow.

A muscle in Gideon's jaw twitched, his face locked in a mask of fiery intensity. "I can't believe I am about to utter these words, but Malaria is needed here. If I'm to lower Tempest into the well, I need someone to watch both our backs."

Steepling her fingers beneath her chin, Ember nodded her understanding. "I appreciate your concerns. Unfortunately, Charlie insists the wedding be rushed. The one thing she doesn't have yet is her gown. If our star designer isn't there to distract her with fabric swatches and beading, Charlie will most certainly come looking for her."

Pulling the rope from his satchel, Gideon lassoed it around his forearm and cast a critical glance down the length of the diminutive witch. "Does that mean you're staying in her place? No offense, but you're pocket-sized."

Hearing the screech of an owl overhead, Ember searched the night sky for traces of her feathered comrade. "I sent for a friend to help. And I do believe he has arrived."

From around the corner of Wake the Dead Coffee came a moonlit shadow that steadily stretched and grew before us. As it swelled to a towering height, it shrugged off its hood to reveal polished bone gleaming in the moonbeams.

"Bones!" I launched myself at him, catching my skeleton friend in an awkwardly intimate bear hug. "Malaria said my sister made a light fixture out of you! How did you break free?"

Since my tight embrace was pinning his arms to his sides, all he could offer was a pat on the back with one bony hand. "Forced to hang there and watch your sister's exploits with the Overly-Friendly Houseguest proved to be all the inspiration I needed to piece myself back together. Soon as I did, I fled the manor. The whole ordeal took time, but that was the one thing I had working in my favor. However, I must admit, I didn't quite know how everything went together. Now, my left foot is pointed in the wrong direction and I often find myself wandering in circles."

"That's okay! I will *gladly* steer you in the right direction." Instead of freeing him from my embrace, I squeezed him harder still.

"I appreciate that, My Queen. I do," he grunted. "However, you have one hand on my vertebra and the other locked on my rib cage. I mean no disrespect, but for a man with no flesh, this is a level of intimacy I'd rather wish we hadn't achieved."

Immediately, I let go and inserted a few feet of distance between us. "Sorry. I'm just so happy you're okay."

Spine straightening, his jawbones clicked together as he adamantly shook his head. "Oh, I'm not okay. Far from it. I'm here to keep you safe as you approach the Rofenod, thereby earning my place by your side for the battle to come against your wretched sibling. There is nothing I want more than to personally tear *your* crown from her curly head and banish her from ever stepping foot in this realm again."

Rolling her eyes, Malaria clucked her tongue against the roof of her mouth. "*That's* the best plan of vengeance you can come up with? She made you into a *light fixture*, for cryin' out loud. You know what? I'm going back to the manor. And when I get there, I'm going to exact a little justice in a *truly* vile way."

"What do you have in mind?" I called after the fashionista, who was already marching in the direction of the manor.

Fist raised in the air, she boomed her battle cry. "I'm putting a giant bow on the ass of her gown, and using clingy fabric that accentuates *every* flaw!"

Glancing my way, Gideon clasped his lips together tightly to fight off a laugh. "Any chance that's the approach that will miraculously chase your sister out of town?"

"No way."

"Then, down the hole you go."

TWELVE

Gideon looped his rope over a neighboring street lantern to prevent it from fraying against the rough edges of the stone when he lowered me down. The other end was lassoed around my hips, just under my butt, to allow me to sit back, place my feet against the wall, and ease myself down in a hand-over-hand grip.

With one knee braced on the top of the well, Gideon hooked one finger under my chin and tipped my face to his. "You remember what I said to do if there is the slightest hint of trouble?"

"I'm trying to remember, but right now all that comes to mind is screaming and openly sobbing." My attempt at a laugh morphed into a whimper.

Shoulders squared, Bones snorted in haughty judgment. "How ridiculous. What do you possibly have to fear? Need I remind you that so-called creature is *your father*? Although he's lived as a monster for years, it's not like he's going to eat you. The worst that could happen is him pummeling you with his freakishly long arms."

Slowly, Gideon turned his attention in the direction of the oblivious skeleton. "If you were trying to help, you missed the mark."

Feet dangling in the dark abyss of the well, I kept one arm locked over the stone wall. "You know, no one likes it when guests drop by unannounced. Maybe I can write him a little note and drop it down. Then, he knows I'm coming and rewards my etiquette by not shredding me to ribbons."

Tightening his hold on the rope, Gideon squatted down to my eye level. "You heard what Ember said, *mo bhanrion*. The wedding is being rushed. If we don't do this now, we might not get another chance. We both know Charlie won't be granted the Legba power upon her wedding. When that fails to happen, I shudder to think of what she will do to the town—and Lugosi—in her enraged disappointment."

"You're right. I know you're right. Not that accepting your logic diminishes my looming sense of dread even slightly." Pressing the balls of my feet on the well wall, my lips sank into a downward C. "Walk me through the cues again."

Standing up, Gideon shook out the slack rope behind him. "Give the rope one tug if you want to stop, and two if you want to be pulled back up. As soon as you reach the bottom, give three tugs to let me know you made it. Got it?"

"It's adorable that you think I'm going to remember how to count when I'm being swallowed whole by inky darkness."

Gideon's pale lips curled into a sweet smile. "Bones is armed with a sword and will watch my back, allowing me to keep my attention focused entirely on you. I give you my word, My Queen, that I won't let anything happen to you."

"How can you promise that when you're up here and I'm dangling in a pit of despair?" I whined.

Grabbing hold of the rope holding me, Gideon swung me to the edge for no other reason than to press a quick kiss to my lips. "Because, Tempest Mortem, in case you haven't caught on yet, I am utterly, completely, and hopelessly in love with you. If I hear so much as a squeak of unease, I will swan dive into that well and carry you out on my back if need be."

Stunned into silence, all I could manage was, "You love me?"

"I do," he confirmed with a resolute nod, strands of platinum hair falling across his forehead.

"You've never said that before."

"I was waiting for the perfect moment. You know, with you dangling over a pit, and a skeleton pretending he's not eavesdropping."

"I'm not, by the way," Bones interjected, keeping his back to us.

I opened my mouth to second the sentiment, only to immediately clamp it shut again. "I want to say it back. I do. But if I uttered that sentiment right now, it would forever feel like it came from a place of blind panic, and you deserve better than that. The second my feet are back on solid ground, we will pick this conversation up where we left off."

Biting his lower lip, Gideon let his hungry gaze sweep over me. "Then I suggest you hurry back. I'm finding myself in need of some long-overdue affirmations."

The skeleton who swore he wasn't listening shook his head, the vertebra in his neck audibly grinding with the motion. "Young people today have to make everything a filthy innuendo. In my day, the show of an ankle was scandalous."

Tilting my head, I peered around my hunky pirate to where Bones stood guard. "Funny thing to hear from a guy who walks around with all his bones hanging out."

Jaw falling slack—either in insult or because he never thought of it that way—Bones's red orb eyes snapped in my direction. The scene would have been comical, had he not immediately stiffened. With two fingers, he pointed in the direction of the Home DeadPot. "We've got movement. Get her down the hole, *now*."

Hands tightening around the rope, Gideon dipped his chin in a nod of confirmation. "You ready?"

"Not for one instant since the second I arrived here, but it's become the way of my afterlife now." With a wiggle, I adjusted the braided rope under me. "What do I do? Push off the wall and jump?"

Gideon's brow furrowed at the sound of leaves crunching in the distance. "Not if you want me to have any kind of control in easing you down. Lean back like you're sitting in a chair, keep your feet to the wall, and walk yourself down as you go."

"I can see one person for sure. No signs of others… yet," Bones alerted us in a gruff whisper, flipping his sword over the back of his hand into an underhand grip.

"Be careful," Gideon warned, his hands moving in a blur of speed as he lowered me down hand over hand.

Fighting the feeling I was falling, I learned the hard way that leaning back even a half-inch too far would threaten to backflip me into oblivion. Hunching forward, I hugged the rope to my chest and pointed my toes to maintain constant contact with the wall. A time or two Gideon's hands must have slipped, hurdling me down in sudden bursts of speed that launched my stomach into my throat.

I wanted to call out to my pirate beau. Ask him to slow down. Check that everything was okay. Yet fear that calling attention to ourselves from something above or below kept my mouth clamped firmly shut.

Risking a peek over my shoulder, I tried to determine how much further I had to go. It was impossible to tell with the only light filtering down from the moon, and heavy darkness crushing in from all sides.

I couldn't see anything more than my hand in front of my face, yet something caused the hair on the back of my neck to stand on end.

Prickles of unease scampered down my spine.

Knots of dread tightened in my gut.

I wasn't alone.

Something was beneath me.

Watching.

Waiting.

Scraping its talons against the stone in eager anticipation.

Needing a minute to think beyond my blind panic, I did as Gideon directed and gave the rope one firm tug.

It didn't slow, or stop, but continued to slide downward at that same steady pace.

Not ready to give up, I tried again with more force than before.

Still no luck. If anything, I seemed to be picking up speed.

"Uh, Gideon?" Taking a risk, I called up in audible terror. "I need to stop. *Gideon*?"

Only silence answered.

Tipping my head back, I squinted in hopes of catching some glimpse of what was happening above. "Gideon, can you hear me?"

It's silly, really, to think I diverted my attention topside while choosing to disregard what lurked beneath for even a moment. I didn't see the black tentacle curl around my ankle. Hadn't a clue I was locked in the clutches of danger… until it tightened around my foot. One fast, hard jerk was all it took to rip me out of the rope harness. I hurtled through darkness, the stone floor of the well rising to meet me. Skull slamming to the ground, my vision swam out of focus. I couldn't die. That much I knew. Yet as a curtain of black crept in at the corners of my vision, a hand-shaped monstrosity loomed above me. One fat splat of saliva dripped from its tongue and streaked down my cheek just as the last thread of my slipping consciousness snapped… and I slipped into sweet oblivion.

THIRTEEN

"Don't let the fear in. Don't let the fear in." With my eyes squeezed shut I repeated the chant, fighting to keep Ember's advice top of mind.

That was easier said than done the instant my lids popped open. With one dark tendril coiled around my ankle, the Rofenod dragged me across the cold, stone floor. Its lone blue eye split down the middle, the pink point of its tongue flopping between razor-sharp teeth that dripped with saliva.

"The fear is in!" I screeched. Curling my fingers into claws, I scrambled for enough traction to slow my approach to unescapable pain and dismemberment. "The fear is all the way in!"

Just as my fingertips caught hold of a groove in the rock, a second tendril snaked around my waist and tore what little grip I had away with one firm tug. Quickly running out of options that didn't involve being chewed on, I threw my weight to the side. Rolling onto my belly, I used both hands and feet to launch into a frantic army crawl in the opposite direction. *"I came here for polite conversation, ya big slobbery freak!"*

A rolling snap of a tentacle and I was flat on my back once more, with the tender spot on the back of my skull throbbing with fresh waves of pain. Shoulders hunched, the creature supported itself on its knuckles, its impossibly long arms planted on either side of my head.

Drops of spit raining down, I covered my head with both arms and fought for clarity through the alarms of panic blaring through my mind. "*Father... you're my father!*"

Unfortunately, the Rofenod decided to forgo any kind of family reunion and devour my flesh instead. Seizing hold of my wrist, it stretched my arm out to the side, its jaws opening wide for their first taste.

As it turned out, that was exactly the motivation I needed to switch my flight mechanism to fight. "Aw, hell no!" Teeth grinding, I called forth the Legba power and cast out a protective veil for one. Iridescent swirls of green and purple sealed around me, knocking the Rofenod back. Its tendrils shrank to its sides, writhing as it was scorched by the contact.

Leaping to my feet, I kept one hand outstretched before me.

I expected him to shriek.

Hiss.

Charge.

Any of those violent traits he exhibited every time we crossed paths.

Instead, he retracted his teeth and blinked my way with that red-rimmed eye. Hand-shaped head tilting, one digit from his skull twitched towards the Veil. With a feather-soft touch, he brushed the surface, marveling at the colors that danced and swirled at the contact. If I didn't know better—and I didn't—I could have sworn that something resembling melancholy turned his eye glassy with agonizing emotion.

It was there.

Something real.

Something human.

I could see it.

Veil held firmly in place, I took a bold step forward. "Legba?"

His gaze snapped in my direction, silver flares of warning sparking in the depths of his stare.

Swallowing hard, I prayed I wasn't making the most idiotic mistake of my existence... and dropped the Veil. "Legba, I know you're in there. Everything you've done has been for your people. I understand that now... and I see you."

Of course I winced when his head fell back in an ear-piercing shriek. Muscles taut, I was ready to run and climb that rope Spiderman-style if need be. But it was the change that occurred in the middle of his screech that kept me rooted where I stood. His beastly bellow morphed into the pained scream of a man.

The jaws of the Rofenod fell open, its monstrous façade peeling back. In a gruesome squish of flesh, all that it was fell in a pooled heap on the ground... at the feet of a handsome black man with one blue eye, one brown eye, and graying hair at his temples. He was dressed in a deep plum tuxedo with a ruffled collar buttoned at his throat.

"Legba." His silhouette was on the twenty-dollar coin in Carnage Crossing, yet that wasn't why he was familiar to me. Since arriving on that macabre little island, the words he scratched into his journal had become my guide, the teaching I followed to learn how to rule and become a queen worthy of my people. Unsure of how one went about greeting an exorcised King, I offered a weird bow/ curtsy/ wave thing. "Your Highness."

A smile as brilliant as the first light of dawn brightened his features. "Tempest..." Proving there were awkward moments even after death, Legba started to raise his arms at his sides, as if welcoming me into his embrace. Hesitating, he dropped them once more and offered me a bow of respect instead. "Queen Tempest Mortem, if anyone was going to see me as myself for even a moment, it's my honor to have it be you."

Sure, his smile stayed plastered in place. Yet even in that dark well, I could see the storm clouds of regret brewing behind his eyes. Not that I blamed him. As far as he knew, the only memories I had of my father were of him abandoning his family.

But Carnage Crossing showed me the truth, and I couldn't be more proud to call Legba my dad. Black-tinged tears filling my eyes, I closed the space between us in four wide strides. Without an ounce of hesitation, I threw myself into his arms.

Folding me into his embrace, his own free-flowing tears dripped into my hair. "Tempest, my sweet Tempest."

His smell—dirt and dried rose petals—made my head swim with a million questions I couldn't begin to vocalize. Memories walled up behind a magical ward scratched and clawed to the surface, bursting free in a rush of bittersweet melancholy.

Voice hoarse with emotion, the truth gushed from my lips in an unstoppable geyser. "Every night, you would light a candle beside my bed and make shadow puppets as you sang me to sleep."

"The song was called *Dodo Titit.*" Emotion made the words catch in his throat. Swallowing hard, Legba pressed a gentle kiss to the top of my head. "It's an old Haitian lullaby. I just prayed you would never find out it was about a crab eating a child."

"I didn't," I laughed through my tears, "but somehow that seems fitting."

The chuckle he gave was a deep boom that shook from his chest. Looking at him now, it would be easy to mistake him for a normal man, at a glance. Yet his demeanor and stature spoke of a strength and power that resonated from his soul. "I suppose that's a plus *and* minus of being in the world of the dead. You're safe from murderous crabs, but are also tragically denied of Kalalou." At my confused frown, he clarified, "That's Haitian gumbo."

Unbeknownst to him, that wasn't the reason for the pained look carved into my features. Countless memories were rushing in, filling blanks in my head and heart that I never knew were there. He taught me how to sail, showing me how to tie strong knots in the rope despite my withering arm. In the ballroom, he would let me stand on his shoes as he waltzed me in circles in time with the music. We walked hand in hand through the Eternal Night

Forest, picking bouquets of wildflowers for my mother. Taking a knee before me, he held up the radiant blooms and explained the flowers were there because of us. That we had brought life and beauty to the island… and his heart.

"We were a family, and we were happy," I sobbed, more to myself than him.

Catching both of my hands in his, Legba clutched them to his chest. "For a sliver of time, we were. That said, if you ask me if I regret sending you all away, I'm afraid you'll be disappointed by my answer. My three girls were my everything. You brought color and vibrance back into a gray, lifeless world. But you were wilting in this place. All of you, in your own devastating ways. I was broken beyond repair after casting you back to the land of the living, yet I never doubted the decision for an instant. It was the right thing to do. With my memories of our time together wrapped around me like a protective shroud, I did what needed to be done to protect my family." Seizing my shoulders, he held me at arm's distance to let his proud, paternal gaze sweep over me. "Seeing you here now is all the affirmation I need to know my choice was a sound one. You have grown into a woman who matches the beauty of her mother while exuding the strong Legba power."

Sucking air through my teeth, I took a step back and dragged my free hand through the tangled mess of my hair. "For sure you made the right decision… *then.* But how much do you know about what's going on *now*?"

Reluctantly pulling away from me, Legba strode deeper into the darkness of the well. I heard a match strike, and a soft glow filled the dank space as he lit a torch. Light played through the cavern, illuminating prized humanly possessions he'd stowed away during his time as the Rofenod.

Books.

Paintings.

Miscellaneous keepsakes.

All situated around the space, adding a homey feel to his otherwise dismal circumstance. All of it acting as proof that beneath the monstrous façade lived a man haunted by the afterlife stolen from him.

Taking a cross-legged seat on the ground, my father gestured for me to join him. "I know that a creature of darkness clawed its way up from below. I tried to warn you any way I could—at the ball and the theater. Unfortunately, as you know, that turned into a far bigger fiasco. Thankfully, your instincts led you to the truth about that traitor without my aid."

Easing myself down onto the chilled stone opposite him, I watched the flicker of flames play across his features and saw bits of Charlie and myself reflected back. My pointy chin matched his, while Charlie could thank him for her curls. "What about since then?"

Lips pursed tight, his chin dropped to his chest. "Crimson has returned. I can feel her presence… and that ever-present darkness rooted in her heart. My plan to free her of it failed."

My gaze swept over Legba's collection, an item barely an arm's length away demanding my attention. The candlestick he made my mother. Picking it up with a delicate touch, I turned it over and found the space left by the missing stone that led me there. "She goes by Charlie now, and somehow she crossed the Veil with her heart still beating away. The things she can do are as astounding as they are terrifying. She found a way to control people and make them into her mindless puppets. Unless—"

"They are marked with the Hamsa hand." Brow furrowed, he scratched at his chin with the knuckle of his index finger. "That explains why she didn't even attempt to target the Rofenod—she couldn't. No doubt she tried. What better way to inflict fear into the hearts of others than to be flanked by a grotesque monster?"

You know when a friend criticizes themself, and you feel inclined to jump in and reassure them that their worst thoughts about themselves aren't true? How was I supposed to offer that same courtesy to a guy who had a hand for a head and teeth in his lone eyeball?

"I would say more off-putting than grotesque." That was my sorry attempt. I knew as soon as it left my mouth that it missed the mark.

Still, Legba saw the remark for what it was and offered a humorless huff of laughter. "Thankfully, your arm healed as intended. It breaks my heart the same couldn't be said for your sister… or mother. I blame myself for all the afflictions you suffered by being here among the dead. Had you not, none of this would have happened. My great mistake was allowing myself to fall in love with Belladonna. But I was enchanted by her graceful beauty and generous heart, and found myself powerless to resist."

"You wanted love and family, just like everybody else. You can't be faulted for that. And when you realized what this place was doing to us, you made what had to be the hardest decision of your existence by turning us away. I appreciate that, and respected it." Carefully setting the candlestick aside, I met Legba's stare and held it. "Unfortunately, hugging it out doesn't change our current situation. The longer Charlie is here, the more twisted and vile her nature will become. Past experience taught us that. We are her blood, so it's up to us to stop her. Or, we'll hold a fair share of the guilt for anyone else she hurts."

Pride crinkled the corners of his mismatched eyes. "Spoken like a true queen."

Hands up, I adamantly argued, "Oh, no. No way. With you here, and not in the form of a shrieking monster, that crown rightfully belongs to you. The people of Carnage Crossing adore you. They'd love nothing more than to see you seated back on your throne where you belong. We just need to work together to make that happen. If you have any suggestions in that regard, I'm all ears. Because short of uncovering the hole where Ambrose dug his way up and yeeting her inside, I've got nothing. And—truth be told—I'm even leery of that idea. Give her five minutes in hell, and I have no doubt Charlie would end up running the place."

Resting his upturned hands on his knees, all trace of emotion vanished from Legba's features. "The answer is already in front of you. To find it, you must focus on the truths as you know them for the island."

Unable to sit calmly at a time like this, I rolled onto my knee and pushed to standing. Wringing my hands, I paced back and forth beneath the opening of the well. "While it is a nice change of pace that your cryptic messages don't rhyme, that doesn't make them any easier to decipher than Ember's. Seeing as people are currently being held hostage by your youngest offspring, is there any chance we could try a more direct approach?"

Lips parting with a pop, Legba's brows knit together in confusion. "The apothecary speaks in rhymes since I entrusted her with the gift of sight? Huh. Maybe it was the wording of the ward I chose? Whatever the case, that was never my intention."

"Fantastic. It's wonderful to know I've been suffering through a glorified typo."

"As for Charlie," he began. Leaning back on his palms, Legba stretched his legs out in front of him and crossed them at the ankle. "I ask again; what are the absolute truths you know about the island?"

"*That's just it*!" Spinning on him, I curled my fingers beside my head as if suppressing the urge to rip my hair out. "Everything I think I know changes all the time! This is a world of the dead, but my very much alive sister just waltzed right in. Oh, and everyone *has* to have a Memento Mori, but my ex-from-hell somehow strolled around without one. The rules change all the time!"

Legba's head tilted in mild interest. "If the boy didn't have a Memento Mori, how did you target him for an exorcism?"

My mouth fell open, the sudden realization that slammed into me knocking the vocabulary clean out of my head. "By being here, an item belonging to him became his Memento Mori... *meaning the same will happen to Charlie.*"

"There it is. Clever girl, just like your mother."

Thoughts turning to my own Memento Mori, I said a silent prayer that someone had the foresight to hide it away before Charlie could use it against me... again. "How do I figure out which item it is? Another visit to The Host? I have to admit, I don't think they liked me very much. The whole *don't look at me or I'll eat your face* rule was a hard one for me to follow. Mostly because they resemble an alien on meth."

Legba's shoulders shook as a shiver raced down his spine. "I don't blame you. I've been surrounded by death for eons, but that thing gives me the creeps. You know, I'm not entirely certain they didn't crash land here. Regardless, we may not need them. Do you happen to know if anyone has given Charlie anything since she arrived?"

Shaking my head, I let one shoulder rise and fall. "As far as I know, from the moment she arrived, she's taken everything by force."

Legba hopped to his feet with ageless agility. "Then everything she's acquired isn't truly hers. That being the case, any item of hers brought here from the living world would act as her Memento Mori. Do you know where she was living before she crossed over?"

My nose crinkled, teeth grinding hard enough to crack a molar. "Of course I do. It's the same place *I* was living before she plotted my death, seduced my fiancé, and tried to erase me from existence. My townhouse. The last time I walked out that door, I swore I would never go back."

"Never is a frightfully long time, child, and I'm afraid we've run out of options."

FOURTEEN

One final grunt and Legba's feet flipped over the edge of the well and sank into the grass, allowing him to shrug off the rope Gideon used to heave him topside.

"That climb is significantly more difficult without tentacles." Glancing at the two men, he offered them both a grin. "Though it *is* nice to see other people without them shrieking and running from me."

His attempt at witty banter was brushed aside by Bones falling to his knees, his skull thrown back to gaze up at Legba's face adoringly. "My King. My liege. It really is you! I had my suspicions, but to truly gaze upon your noble glory—"

"Whoa, whoa, whoa!" Palms out, I pumped the brakes on this conversation moving even a millimeter further. "You weren't sure it was him *before* you dropped me down the hole? It would have been nice to know beforehand that we were betting on a theory!"

For a guy with no skin or muscles, Bones's sass alone made the transition from adoration to annoyance clear as his head lolled in my direction. "If I had told you, you wouldn't have gone."

"None of that matters now." Seizing his Vizier by the forearm, Legba hoisted him to his feet. Together they shared one of those manly bro-hugs where they seized each other tight and pounded their fists on each other's back hard enough to knock teeth loose. "It's been too long, brother."

"All this time," Bones's voice cracked, rising and falling with threatening tears, "you've been here, looking out for your people the only way you could."

Pulling his longtime ally back to an arm's length, Legba gave Bones's gaunt shoulder a final pat before releasing him. "Don't give me too much credit in that regard. The screaming and wailing of that monstrous mind overtook me more than I care to admit. I saw clarity in flashes through a beastly fog. The rest of the time… I mostly wanted to pick people up and toss them around."

Picking up my mask from where I set it beside the Screaming Well, I balanced it on my hip. "That sounds so much more playful than what I thought you had in mind."

One arm pressed to his chest, Bones bent deeply in a bow of respect. "Sire, Carnage Crossing needs you more than ever. If anyone can vanquish the threat facing us, it's you."

With a snort, I bumped Gideon's elbow with mine. "Can you believe this guy? I mean, Legba is a king… not a deity."

In place of a response, Gideon dropped to his knees and presented his dagger to Legba by the hilt. "My King, I have committed an egregious offense against you. I pledged vows to your daughter, swore my afterlife and very existence to her… all without your consent. Flog me. Exorcise me. Banish me, if it pleases you. I deserve whatever punishment you see fit for stealing the hand of your eldest daughter."

"Really?" I mumbled. "You too?"

Legba eased the blade towards the ground and gestured for Gideon to rise. "You did what you thought was right to ensure the crown went to the rightful heir. As long as you are true to her—and behave like a gentleman—this union has my blessing."

Rolling my eyes, I clucked my tongue against the roof of my mouth. "Are we all done fangirling over my dad? Need I remind you that Charlie is carving out a throne for herself on the backs of the people we care for? And what was the ruckus up here that dropped me right into the Rofenod's arms?"

"Charlie has Sparrow out on patrol." Gideon dragged his fingers through his hair, revealing fresh claw marks on his forearm. "We tried to hold her down long enough to mark her, but that woman is surprisingly scrappy. Granted, I only had one hand to hold her, but she slipped right from our grasp. As horrible as it sounds to say, at least Charlie keeps her in a mindless state. She won't be reporting back about anything."

"Undoubtedly, Legba has a *brilliant* plan to stop Charlie." Positioning himself at my father's elbow, Bones peered at his king in hopeful expectation. "So, what's our play?"

"Step one?" Jabbing my free hand on my hip, I lifted one brow. "That would be for you to climb out of my father's ass so you can actually be helpful."

"What a horrifying visual," Bones deadpanned.

"You'll have to excuse my daughter. She's using sarcasm as a defense mechanism because she doesn't want to venture back to her townhome, as I suggested." Legba's brows raised in challenge, daring me to argue.

Chin to my chest, that comment earned my most sour look. "Not sure you know me well enough to call me out like that."

Knowing all too well my loathing for that particular piece of real estate, Gideon bristled by my side. "Why would that be advisable… or necessary?"

Clearing my throat, I struggled to achieve a somewhat casual tone. "I need to find something of Charlie's we can use as her Memento Mori."

Other than the tendons in his tightly clenched jaw flexing, Gideon's handsome face remained eerily absent of emotion. "I mean no disrespect, My King, but the cracks in the Veil can't be ignored. How do we know it's stable enough for her to venture across and safely return?"

Tugging the lapels of his coat to smooth them into place, Legba held his head high. "We have nothing to fear there. I will take it upon myself to hold the Veil open to ensure her safe passage."

Tentatively, Bones raised one bony hand to signal he had a question. "While it pains me to say it, we have no idea how long you will stay in this form, My King. What if you morph back to the Rofenod while Tempest is still on the other side?"

"Well, the lass can maneuver the Veil on her own." Legba gave a one-shoulder shrug. "She should be able to handle matters herself if need be. Plus, she broke the ward I was trapped in by acknowledging me as the man I truly am. It's fair to assume the two of you could do the same."

Lips sinking into a downward C, I drummed my fingernails against my mask. "Not loving words like *should*, *assume*, and *could* being used in a plan to prevent me from being trapped for all eternity in the land of the living."

"Then you're *really* going to hate this next part." Gideon grimaced, shoving his hands into the pockets of his slacks. "You're going after a Memento Mori, which hints at using it to exorcise Charlie. Unfortunately, she's marked with the Hamsa hand… and she's still alive."

Silence fell, all of us marinating in the two huge flaws we'd overlooked.

"We're usually better at this," I stage-whispered to Legba, shifting my weight from one foot to the other. "Let's call it what it is… performance anxiety."

Stare drifting to the cracks in the Veil zigzagging across the sky, Legba spoke with the wisdom of centuries. "You cannot exorcise the living. Her spirit would merely be banished from this land, forcing her back beyond the Veil."

"And the Hamsa hand?" I pressed, seeing that mark as the huge stop sign it was.

Peaceful resignation softened my father's features, a hint of a smile playing at the corners of his lips. "Leave that to me."

FIFTEEN

"Question: once I get what we need out of here, if I were to—oh… say—burn this place to the ground, would it burn in the living world, too?" Staring up at the brick two-story I once called home, all I saw it as now was a reminder of every bad thing that had gone down here since.

Legba's mouth opened to answer, only to immediately snap shut again. "I have no idea. No one has ever wanted to sever the ties to the life they left behind enough to turn to arson."

With his fingertips brushing the small of my back, Gideon whispered against my ear. "One last time. Then we'll strike that match together."

Swiveling on the ball of his foot, my father planted himself in front of me and caught my hands in his. "For the sake of safety, and due to the uncertainty as to how long I'll be in this form, you mustn't dawdle. Grab the first item you're certain belongs to Charlie, then hurry out."

"Really?" Head cocked, I blinked up at him as if perplexed by that directive. "I was planning to order a pizza and stream all the shows I'm behind on before I sashayed out."

Bones jerked, aghast I would suggest such a thing. "That's ludicrous! Time is of the essence! This is no time for loafing and indulgence!"

Tossing my mask to Gideon, I combed my fingers through my hair before twisting it up and out. I fastened it into place with a ribbon of fabric I tore from one of Gideon's shirts during one of our nights in the cave. "If you don't like my methods, may I suggest that *I* stay out here and cast unnecessary judgments while *you* venture inside?"

Chin lifting with a condescending air, Bones crossed his spindly arms over his rib cage. "I absolutely would take up such a yoke for my king… but I'm not familiar with Charlie, nor her belongings."

"Funny, since up until recently you were one of them," I jabbed back. "Tell me, during your time as a light fixture, did she dust you? Give you a little spit polish?"

"Enough!" Legba boomed. "Bones, I'm fairly certain my daughter was—as the kids say—messing with you. All in an attempt to procrastinate from the task at hand." The brow over his blue eye lifted in a challenge for me to argue otherwise.

"I'm going, but before I do…" I held up one finger. "Are we all sure we don't want to burn off our Hamsa marks and just resign ourselves to being Charlie's sock puppets? I mean, it does seem like it would be a lot less stressful."

Vacant stares were the only response.

"No?" I let my raised hand fall open, palm up. "Alright fine, I'll go arm us for the war to come. But if something or someone in there exorcises me, I'm finding a way to claw my way back from the abyss just to haunt all three of you."

I made it as far as the front steps when Legba called after me, "And I'm sure we will be thrilled to see you… in between the chain rattling and bellows from the beyond."

While Bones openly snorted with laughter, Gideon had the foresight to hide his amusement behind his hand.

"You're all going to feel really bad if that's the last thing anyone ever said to me," I muttered to myself. Jogging up the stairs,

I reached for the doorknob, knowing it would swing open on its own. It did not disappoint. Darkness beckoned me inside, eerie silence lurking in every corner and crevice. No sooner did I step over the threshold, than the door slammed shut behind me… and locked. "That's new… and off-putting."

"I knew you would come."

Enough time had passed since The Houseguest invaded my mind, I jumped at the sound of his voice, my hands curling into defensive fists at my sides.

"Even without my guidance, I had no doubt instinct would lead you here."

Venturing into the front room, I noticed the thick layer of dust that had settled over the framed pictures of Charlie and Ambrose lining the bookshelves. "And where are you? Sulking in the walls like the creeper you are? Or back at the manor, glossing your lips so you can kiss every square inch of my sister's ass?"

Laughter echoed down the hall, chasing prickles down my spine. This was no mind game. I wasn't alone.

No longer was his voice confined to the walls of my mind. It followed me down the hall. Greeted me from doorways. Beckoned me to venture further… as if herding me. To where, I didn't know.

"I've been impressed with you since you first arrived here. How you latched onto Lugosi, instinctively understanding the importance of allies in a world you didn't understand."

I peeked into the bathroom in the hall, only for the door to slam shut in my face. Passing a framed eight by ten photo of Charlie and Ambrose hand in hand in Central Park, I blinked and saw Ambrose's face morph to the demon he became. Steps slow and cautious, I inched my way to the kitchen. Cabinet doors swung open and shut. Cutlery shook in the clapping drawers.

"And when I saw the charge you led here? Waves of ghouls flooding in to torment the living? It was mastery defined. Nothing short of a chef's kiss. I may have been entombed in the walls, but even I *couldn't help but play along."* As if to prove the part he played, a hand stretched out of the wall beside me, swiping at the air between us.

Steps quickening, I darted towards the TV room at the back of the house. Ever since we were kids, Charlie had a quilt our mother made her that she snuggled up with whenever she watched TV. If it was there, I could grab it and make a fast getaway.

Of course, that's not how it went.

The TV clicked on as soon as I stepped into the room, my own face appearing on the screen. Head tilting, the televised version of me offered a vacant smile as torrents of blood gushed from the wound in my throat that claimed my life.

"*This is your chance, Tempest. The opportunity to end the war before it even begins. I follow power, and in this moment, I bow to you.*"

A lightbulb popped overhead, raining shards of glass into the carpet. "Why now? You've lapped up the Kool-Aid at Club Charlie since Lugosi freed you. What would make your loyalty shift now?"

The television clicked off.

All slamming doors stilled.

Silence fell.

The only response I received came from one lone light clicking on over the staircase that led to the second floor.

"One thing that can be said for the dead; they are masters in the art of subtlety." Doing my best to ignore the icy dread creeping through my sluggish veins, I tiptoed upstairs.

I can't say what exactly I expected to find.

Never in the wildest scenarios did I anticipate rounding the corner into the master bedroom to find Charlie lying in the middle of the bed. Yet, there she was. Dressed in a long, white lace nightgown, her hands gently folded over her chest. A halo of curls encircled her head as her chest rose and fell in shallow breaths.

"I'll save you some time. Your sister mastered the art of astral projection."

Jumping at the sound of his voice directly behind me, I spun in time to see The Friendly Houseguest seeping from the wall. The smile he offered may have been welcoming, if his entrails weren't dripping black sludge onto the carpet in heavy splats.

"She's in both places at once? How?" I asked, forcing myself to keep focused on his face to avoid the mess happening from the waist down.

"The idea came from your mother's journal." He jerked his chin in the direction of the book on the nightstand. "While darling Belladonna hunted for a way to cross over and reunite with her lover, she was never successful. Yet somehow little sister tweaked mother's ideas and is now simultaneously napping *and* stealing your kingdom. She's quite the multi-tasker."

Stepping closer to the edge of the bed, I traced my mother's handwriting on the front of the notebook. "You speak of Charlie with such reverence, but here you are. Why would you change teams in the third quarter?"

Easing down on the mattress beside Charlie—and creating a puddle of nastiness beneath him no detergent could ever get out—The Houseguest lovingly dragged one knuckle across Charlie's cheek. "Your sister is quite the specimen, and I have thoroughly enjoyed our time together. However, as I caught glimpses through the walls of what you were up to, I had to scurry over for a tête-á-tête. Power is my drug and at the moment," his hungry gaze shifted my way, his pupils dilated with desire, "you have it in spades."

Chewing on the inside of my cheek, I fought to keep my expression neutral. "Why now?"

His back ramrod straight, he lifted a hunk of his lower intestine and crossed one leg over the other. "Because this is the moment when everything can change."

A spark of hope ignited in my core, casting waves of warmth through me. "Then the plan to grab one of her possessions as a Memento Mori will work? We're on the right track?"

As if he smelled something truly foul, The Houseguest's face crumbled. "*That's* your plan? Rather pathetic, really. I expected more from you."

"Thanks for not sugarcoating it to spare my feelings."

"Why would I? Opportunity is staring you in the face." He jabbed both hands in Charlie's direction. "Here lies your sister, completely vulnerable. No one but the two of us even knows she's here... were anything to happen to her."

Not liking the dark turn this was taking one iota, I took a step back. Then another. "And you're suggesting I do what, exactly?"

"Suggesting?" Surprised by my word choice, his head jerked. "I think I've made it blatantly obvious. Out there, in Carnage Crossing, all the cards are stacked in Charlie's favor. You stand no chance if you go up against her. How could you? She'll have your people tear you apart while she sits back and watches. Right here, right now, you could end it all and take back the throne. Chase life from Carnage Crossing and restore your reign of divine decay."

If I said I wasn't tempted, I would be lying. It would be so simple to take the pillow from beneath her head and hold it over her face until her body gave the last twitch of life... and stilled. But, in spite of everything she'd done, she was still my sister. The same curly-haired pain in my ass who climbed in bed and cried herself to sleep with her head on my shoulder after Mitch Connor broke her heart. The same grass-stained kid who came limping in the house after falling off her bike and skinning her knee when Mom wasn't home. I dressed wounds. Dried tears. Threatened bullies. Chased off dirtbag guys. A million different moments, thousands of instances, of me caring for her in the way only a big sister can.

I realized now I never really knew Charlie or what she was capable of, but I knew who I became because of her. Someone who cared. Someone who helped. Someone who chose to be selfless when the situation called for it. No way in hell was I going to allow her to make me something I wasn't, simply because it was the easier option.

"And if I don't?" I rasped, green and purple wisps licking up my arms.

Knuckles mashed into my mattress, The Houseguest pushed himself to his feet. "Ugh, what a frightfully boring alternative.

If you must know, if you don't end her now you will leave me no choice but to scurry back to her metaphysical side and tell her all about this little plan of yours to exorcise someone who isn't even dead. Kudos to you on thinking outside the box with that, by the way, though it's slightly idiotic. One way or the other, I'll stand by the side of the greater power. It's up to you to decide if you'd rather have me as an ally… or an enemy."

He didn't know about Legba. He couldn't, or he definitely would have mentioned that little nugget of afterlife-altering info. It made sense if he could only move through walls. The Rofenod's makeshift home was at the bottom of the Screaming Well, and the only other place we had been was outside. Guest had no clue the King who banished him had returned, and I intended to keep it that way.

Sauntering to my dresser that now overflowed with Charlie's possessions, I scanned the top of it—and what was poking out of the drawers—for something that would serve the purpose that brought me there. "What makes you think I would ever trust you enough to allow you in my inner circle?"

A devilish chuckle shook his shoulder, his exposed entrails slapping together with the motion. "Trust has nothing to do with it. What I can do, the information I can obtain, holds immeasurable value for a seated queen."

Sliding a sea glass vase aside, I found exactly what I needed. Leaned against Charlie's walnut tree of life jewelry box was her burlap voodoo doll. The real one. Her corporeal body wasn't really in Carnage Crossing, and neither was the doll. She was manipulating the essence of its magic through the power of her mind… a truly terrifying concept.

Plucking the doll from the dresser, I stuffed it in my back pocket as discreetly as I could as I turned to face The Houseguest. "I tell you what – how about if you and I make a deal instead?"

Arms folding across his middle, he hitched one brow in mild interest. "Such as?"

"You stay out of this, and I won't have you exorcised the second this is over." I spoke the words not in threat, but genuine fact.

Black ooze seeping through his teeth, his cracked lips coiled into a malicious smile. "You aren't getting this, are you? I saw that little trinket you stowed away. You weren't nearly as sly about it as you'd like to think. In any event, it won't do you any good. Because you aren't the only one who has been planning and plotting, and—let's face it—little sister is way better at it than you." Dropping his hands into fists at his sides, The Guest took a threatening step closer. "Would you like to know what she's been up to while you've been bumbling around trying to reclaim your throne? She found out about those little marks you've been carving into people and has handled them accordingly."

Fingernails of dread dragged up my spine. "What? *How*?"

It would have been glorious to see The Guest as the handsome piece of eye candy Charlie saw him as for even a moment, as opposed to the grisly ghoul gleefully clucking his gray tongue against the roof of his mouth. "Of course I had to report to Her Majesty on the treachery and whispers I saw and heard through town. The worst offender being that little witch at the apothecary shop. She was marking whomever she could get ahold of. Charlie wasted no time concocting a delicious punishment."

Darkness threatened the edges of my vision. "Which was…?"

His gaze focused on my face, eager to drink in my reaction. "Ember is locked in a room at the Dead End Resort. And, since she tried to bring down Charlie's reign with tiny slices in the flesh of residents, she gets to endure the same. Every hour on the hour, one fresh cut is delivered. But that's not even the best part."

I forced the words through clenched teeth. "What is?"

Throwing his hands in the air, he made the grand reveal. "The person delivering them, of course! Ember marked her love, as one would expect. So, when Charlie learned of how she was sneaking around breaking people free from her thrall, she made an example out of the couple. She allowed me the pleasure of carving Vesper's mark off of him. His screams were deafening, until Her Highness jabbed a pin into the head of her doll to silence him. Once he was back to being a puppet she could manipulate, she gave him a job. Now, whenever the grandfather clock chimes the hour, he ambles in and cuts the woman he loves without the luxury of free will or hesitation." While I boiled in rage over this revelation, he rambled on. "Now, marked or not, the others have fallen in line out of fear of what will happen to them, or those they care for."

For a minute I stared at him, chewing on all the horrors he'd revealed. In that instant, more than anything, I wanted all this to be over, but I refused to grant either him or Charlie even one more win. Instead, I sauntered over and clamped a hand on Houseguest's cold, clammy shoulder. "When this is over, I will show you no mercy. I will see to it you are entombed forever in the deepest, darkest pit with no hope of escape. That, you can bet on." As I uttered the words, I peeled the Veil back over The Friendly Houseguest. Air rippled around him, yet his outward appearance didn't change… for me.

Glancing down at his hands, he gave a sharp bark of laughter. "Was that supposed to be a taste of your power, *former* Queen Tempest? It leaves a bit to be desired… like actual results of any kind."

Turning on my heel, I marched out the door, once more marveling at the misery that awaited each and every time I stepped foot inside that townhouse. "You weren't meant to see a change," I muttered to myself as I jogged down the stairs. "But Charlie will. Good luck getting close enough to tell her *anything* when you look like roadkill, you backstabbing prick."

SIXTEEN

Mask cast aside, my willingness to hide was gone. If Charlie wanted to come for me, let her. That much-needed confrontation between us was long overdue.

As I marched down Croaking Lane with determined strides, Bones, Gideon, and Legba powerwalked to keep up. "I'm done with Charlie and her games. This all ends tonight. She's making Vesper torture Ember! What kind of sick, deranged mind even comes up with that kind of thing? I mean, even when we save her—and you can bet your ass we will—how can their relationship heal from this? She's going to flinch every time he touches her, and for good reason!" Green and purple energy curled from my arms, the air around me crackling with my barely concealed rage. Judging by the darkened edges of my vision, I assumed some of my more ghoulish attributes had taken over. Not that I cared. At that moment, a monstrous façade seemed fitting. "And do you know what the worst part is?"

"That you still haven't told us if you acquired one of her possessions?" Legba interjected, his tone the same practiced calm

I used in the CCU whenever things went from bad to *page the doctor*.

Fighting back the urge to find a colorful way to suggest he go have an illicit love affair with himself, I pulled the voodoo doll from my pocket and held it up for the trio behind me to see. "As it happens, I got her weapon of choice. The real one. Not the trick of her mind version she's been torturing us with. Turns out both she and that creepy burlap *thing* are astral projections haunting *us*. The living is *literally* haunting the dead."

"Weapon of choice?" Face a question mark, Legba glanced to Bones for clarification.

"Apologies, sire, that we failed to explain." Bones dragged his leg with the backwards foot along as fast as he could to match the pace of the other men. "Your youngest daughter has been using a voodoo doll to control the residents of Carnage Crossing."

"And she brought this item here with her?"

"The day she arrived, yes. Or so we thought." Even I heard the clipped nature of the Royal Vizier's tone, as if pondering why his king would get hung up on such a trivial detail.

"Huh," Legba mused in a lighthearted manner that nearly sent me spiraling over the edge. "Then it's a good thing the doll was never truly here."

That was it, folks. Something in my head snapped, causing me to spin on my father. "*How*? How can that possibly be viewed as a good thing? She did all of this with her mind alone! Do you understand the kind of power it takes to not only achieve, but to *maintain* this?"

Bones brought one bony fist to his mouth.

Gideon's wide eyes lobbed from me to Legba and back again.

While both seemed to fear that they were about to see an epic royal clash, Legba kept his voice calm and soothing. "Because if the doll was really here, it would have made your trip to the townhouse and any item you pulled out completely useless. It being in her possession would have automatically made it her Memento

Mori, which I would have told you had you mentioned it. So, as I said, good thing they are merely astral projections."

Rapidly blinking, I let my jaw swing slack. "For the sake of my mental well-being, we're not going to talk about that. Or the *insanely* narrow margin that prevented us from making a colossal mistake."

"The worst part?" Legba pressed.

Chewing on my lower lip, I rubbed my hand over my forehead. "Probably knowing I would have charged right in there thinking I had the upper hand, only to have my ass handed to me."

Rocking in my direction, Gideon bumped my arm with his. "I think we were referring to the situation with Ember, love."

With a shake of my head, I tried to shrug off our potential flub-up. "She's a seer, and a hell of a good one. I have no doubt that she saw this coming. She knew of the pain and agony heading her way, and she—"

"Allowed it to happen," Legba cut in, his stare drifting to the Dead End Resort. "How many times have you witnessed her using the information she has to manipulate the outcome of things? Yet, she didn't do that this time. What does that tell you?"

Heavy clouds hung overhead, yet even they couldn't stifle the hope that came with the dawn of a new day. "She wanted everyone to know the power of the mark, and the lengths Charlie would go to in order to prevent its spread."

He nodded along as if patiently waiting for me to catch up. "Knowing our people as you do, how do you think they responded to that?"

"By carving a mark onto every single person."

"That would be my guess as well. And that plays in our favor." Pride crinkled the corners of his eyes. "You remind me so much of myself. Ready to march into battle without a moment's hesitation. But what we need right now is strategy. Something significant to shake things up… like rendering the Hamsa hand mark completely useless."

I blinked once… and again, trying to determine if he was joking. If so, I definitely didn't get the humor in it. "Uh… you don't see the critical flaw in that plan? That mark is the only thing protecting us from Charlie's influence. We've established that. Repeatedly. Even if we did know of a way to take away its power, why would we want to? That seems like a giant leap in the wrong direction."

"Oh!" Bouncing on the balls of his bleached bone feet, Bones clapped his hands together. "I see what you're hinting at, my lord! Tempest can't use the doll to banish Charlie, because she's protected by the mark. And Tempest can't destroy the mark without putting everyone on the island at risk of falling under Charlie's malicious influence."

"Yes, that is what I was getting at. Not sure I would have jumped and clapped about it, though."

Dropping his hands in front of him, Bones stilled. "Apologies, My King."

Brow furrowed, I ran my thumbs over the voodoo doll's button eyes. I didn't want to utter the words, but Legba was right. The mark had to be destroyed. There was no other way. "We would have to move quickly. Break the ward, then immediately cast Charlie out. If she's given even a sliver of opportunity, she could turn an army of our own people against us. But when? How?"

"She has to pull herself out of the projection on occasion, doesn't she?" Gideon searched my face in search of certainties I couldn't give. "I mean, she's still alive, and it's been days since her arrival. There have to be moments she returns to her body to meet basic mortal needs: food, water, bathroom breaks. If we can pinpoint one such moment, we could remove the ward and be ready to cast her out the second she returns to the realm. What about The Houseguest? He could alert us when to act."

"*He*," I clarified with one finger raised, "is most definitely *not* on our side. But Mel and Lugosi are. They may have some idea of her habits or times of day she's known to be noticeably absent. We find that out, and we can identify the best time to—" My words were cut off by the clang of bells ringing from Catastrophe Tower.

Legba blanched.

Bones's mouth fell open.

Gideon took a protective step closer to my side.

Vigorously rubbing my hands over my face, I tried not to let my mind immediately spiral to a bad place. "Despite having never heard those bells before, is there *any* chance they signify something positive? Like the start of recess? Or the arrival of an ice cream truck?"

"In this case, that is a resounding no." Adjusting his grip on the sword he held at his hip, Bones softened his knees into a battle-ready pose.

"The bells are rung the morning of a royal wedding," Legba explained, regret slathered onto each word. "Which means our planning and plotting is for naught."

"We're out of time." Wetting my lips, I locked stares with my father. "You said you have an idea of how to break the Hamsa hand ward. How certain are you that you can do that?"

One corner of my father's mouth tugged back in a wry smirk. "I feel putting an actual percentage on it would hurt morale more than help it right now."

"That's comforting." I rolled my eyes not at him, but at our complete inability to catch a break. "Bones, Gideon, I'm trusting you two to set Vesper and Ember free. I don't want either of them to hurt even a moment longer. My father and I will head to the manor."

Lacing his fingers with mine, Gideon pressed a kiss to the back of my hand. "I will do as you command, *mo bhanrion*. But before I do, I need your assurance you won't take any unnecessary risks. If I am to leave your side, I need to know you'll be safe."

Palm up, I gestured in my father's direction. "Hey, I have *the* Papa Legba at my side. What could possibly go wrong?"

"Quite a lot, actually," Bones pointed out, his sword held in a two-handed grip in front of him. "I mean, the young lady you're going up against was inadvertently behind the exorcism that turned Legba into the Rofenod, *and* she was directly responsible for Tempest taking a planchette to the trachea. As track records go, neither of you have a superb one against her."

Any trace of emotion vanished from Gideon's features. "You know, sometimes silence isn't just golden… it's appreciated."

"I mean, come on! What are the chances she'll do any of those things to us *again*?" Yes, that was my attempt to make my beau feel better. I realize now my efforts fell tragically short.

Shoulders sinking, Gideon gave a resigned sigh. "That… was far from encouraging."

Taking a bold step forward, Legba seized Gideon's forearm in a gesture of solidarity. "You have my word I will not leave her side. I was not there for her in life, but in death, we are bonded. Go with confidence to fulfill your Queen's command, knowing I will protect her at all cost."

"I'll be back quick as I can. Promise me you'll be careful." With Bones's hand on his shoulder, Gideon reluctantly peeled himself away, venturing in the direction of the resort.

"You know me, the poster child of cautious planning!" I called after him, waving a hand over my head to see him off.

Legba's rough, calloused hand linked with mine and gave a gentle squeeze of comfort. "You did good steering him off."

"And you're a liar," I stated without an ounce of malice, my gaze shifting in my father's direction. "We both know chances are slim *both* of us will walk out of this."

"I know. But if we confessed that to them, they never would have left."

SEVENTEEN

At the edge of the yard leading to Legba Manor, hidden by black rose bushes, Legba and I watched guests file into the grand foyer. All were dressed in their best—with flowing gowns, fitted tuxedos, and extravagant hats—yet the mood was far from celebratory. The crowd ambled inside, wearing somber expressions more fitting for a funeral. In some ways, that was exactly what this was. The death of free will, and the afterlife as they knew it.

Heel bouncing with nervous energy, I glanced in my father's direction. "I've never crashed a wedding… or overthrown a matriarchy before. Any idea where we start? Is there a protocol for this kind of thing?"

Parting the leaves to see better, Legba caught a thorn in the thumb and stuck it in his mouth to clean off the black pearl of sludge that bubbled from the wound. "Can't say I have any experience in this myself. Looks like we're both learning as we go and hoping for the best."

"And here I was worried we wouldn't get any father/ daughter bonding moments."

Catching hold of my wrist, Legba pulled me further down the row of foliage, his index finger pressed to his lips. "Shhh... someone is coming."

Sinking low to the ground, we fell silent, praying our mission wasn't over before it even began. A voice wafted in, getting louder with each footfall that drew it closer. Instantly recognizing that sharp, cutting tone, my chin fell to my chest in relief.

"She told me she wanted her wedding colors to be emerald and *iridescent*. Iridescent is not a color. At best, it's an adjective used to *describe* a color." Malaria rounded one of the marble pillars at the edge of the garden, pulling up short when she spotted us. "No-no-no-no-*no*! You can't be out here in the open like this! If she sees you—"

The words died on her lips as her gaze swiveled to Legba. Any trace of emotion vanished from her features, blatant awe widening her eyes. "My King?" Her stare snapped back to me. "You did it, Tempest. *You really did it.*"

"You know, if you're capable of plowing ahead whilst running your mouth, the absolute *least* you could have done was help me carry the food." Arms full of a mountain of boxes, Enyo appeared behind the fashion designer, nearly slamming into her. "Whoa! Why are we stopped? Are you actually going to help me? Did you finally find that one shred of basic human decency you bury deep beneath bitchy comments and layers of satin?"

Malaria offered no explanation, but hiked up the skirt of her black silk gown enough to kneel before her king.

That's when Enyo saw him. Her eyes immediately filled with black-tinged tears. "My... King?" she stammered, searching both our faces for answers. "How?"

Fearing she would drop her cargo and be forced to face Charlie's wrath, I relieved Enyo of her stake of boxes. "That is a long, rather freaky story. To summarize? He was the Rofenod. Now he's not. We aren't sure if the change is permanent, or how long it will last."

Clapping her fist over her heart, Enyo dipped in a deep curtsy to her king. "Carnage Crossing needed him, and the King returned. I can't wait to see you boot that curly-haired chick out of here. She puts the 'dick' in dictator."

Pushing to her feet, Malaria brushed the grass and dirt from her dress. "It won't be easy. Truthfully, I'd be happier to have the Rofenod make a guest appearance."

Lips pursed, Legba scratched at the scruff on his chin. "I'm going to try not to take that personally."

Hearing the voice of a passerby echoing across the lawn, Malaria caught Legba's sleeve and led us further from sight. "I simply mean Charlie has been an absolute terror. It would have been incredibly rewarding to see her go toe-to-toe with an actual monster. That not being the case, what exactly is the plan?"

Tucking a lock of hair behind my ear, I exchanged awkward glances with Legba. "We don't have one, per se, but I expect things to spiral pretty quickly once we walk through the door."

Both women blinked in our direction, digesting what I said.

"So, you're just going to saunter in… like this?" Malaria waved a hand in the direction of our current ensembles; Legba in his velvet tux, me in a ruffled collar shirt I borrowed from Gideon and a pair of form-hugging black pants. Truth be told, I'd been wearing the same thing for days and was well aware I was smelling spicy.

"Yeah, that's not going to work." Enyo's wild mane of hair brushed her shoulder blades as she shook her head. While Malaria went with the simplistic black gown, the chef showed her flare with a deep plum-colored masterpiece with a sweetheart neckline and full skirt. "We've marked as many people as we could, but there are still those who are very much under Charlie's influence and would attack on sight. Surprisingly, the most violent of them is Sparrow."

"That… is in no way surprising." Legba sucked air through his teeth. "I would prefer not to go up against her in any way."

"We don't want to hurt our own," I added for him.

"That," my father confirmed with a crisp nod. "More to the point, I'm the one who taught her the ways of the sword, and I know all too well that her skills there quickly surpassed my own. I would have to pull back the Veil and lock her with rigor just to avoid anyone being harmed."

"There is another way." One arm across her midsection, Malaria rested the opposite elbow on her hand, her fingertips fiddling with the silver-dollar-sized ruby strung from her neck. "Marked or not, people are scared. They've seen what Charlie can do, and what happens to those who stand against her. They want her off the throne and out of Carnage Crossing. You show them there's a chance we can rise together and actually win? I have no doubt they'll fight beside you in whatever way you need."

"For that to happen, you have to get further than the front door, which you stand no chance of doing, looking like that." Enyo's finger flicked up and down the length of me. "You're going to need to be dressed for the occasion, with your identities concealed… after a much-needed bath. Because I am downwind of you, and *damn*."

"That odor is you?" Legba winced and checked the bottom of his shoe. "I legitimately thought I stepped in something."

Hands raised, I pumped the brakes on the insults. "Hey! I've been trying to save the island. There hasn't been time for primping."

"Oh, we're going to make time." Closing her eyes, Malaria sighed with delight. "Finally, a chance to flex my talent. That sister of yours has the fashion sense of a caution cone. Granted, we don't have a lot of time. But I have some fantastic pieces back at the shop that will be perfect for the occasion."

Despite our dire situation, I huffed a humorless laugh. "Dressing for a coup? That may be the most Carnage Crossing thing we've ever done. Absolutely, I'm in."

EIGHTEEN

In the past, Malaria blended femininity with strength in what she created for me by adding elements of armor to otherwise graceful designs. This time, she concocted a masterpiece of regal power. My gown was made entirely of silver chainmail, with polished plates around my neck, upper arms, and hugging my waist. Hair pinned into a faux chin-length bob, my identity was hidden by a matching chainmail mask that hung from my ears to hide the lower half of my face and the telltale hole in my throat.

While Legba's mask matched mine, Malaria chose a more conventional suit for him. While she stuck with his preferred velvet tux, she changed it out for simple black with a crimson ruffle-collared shirt beneath. The look was pulled together by one owl feather—dyed a deep, cherry red—tucked into the band of his top hat.

With our heads down and attention on high alert, Malaria's fashions allowed us to blend with the masses and stroll right into Legba Manor.

"Look at that," I grumbled, the chain of my mask jangling as I shook my head. "Charlie is as petty as she is cruel."

Offering me his arm, Legba placed his hand gently over mine when I accepted. "How so?"

"The Christmas-inspired décor?" With a lift of my chin, I gestured to the white-sprayed evergreens that filled the foyer with the heady scent of pine. Their branches were draped with black lace and adorned with silver, purple, and green bulbs. "According to Malaria, Charlie took that idea from Mel, Lugosi's betrothed. It was based on a story about a spider that his grandmother used to tell him. See the spiderwebs painted on each of the bulbs? Straight from the lore. She stole his love *and* misappropriated his culture."

Brow creased with disgust, Legba guided me down the hall towards the throne room. "Some siblings squabble over borrowed clothing and nasty attitudes. Yet here you are, trying to prevent yours from being a plague against mankind."

Heels clicking over the marble floor, we passed through the stained-glass *C.C.* doors arm in arm. It was plain to see at a glance why the entire town had been so eerily quiet. Countless people must have been wrangled in to help orchestrate this elaborate affair on such a short amount of time. Neat rows of chairs were covered in sheer black fabric. On the back of each, tied in a matching bow, was a spray of sticks and one branch of Douglas fir with a single pine cone. Pillar candles of every size lined the aisle, flickering a gentle welcome to the altar waiting at the end. The altar itself was constructed out of deep walnut with bows tied with the same black fabric as the chairs. A beautiful arrangement of red roses and pine was knotted at the peak, spilling down the sides.

I would have found it lovely, were it not for my sister's sinister intentions. "She wasn't always like this," I said as much for my own benefit as Legba's. "Before she found our mother's journal, she seemed genuinely happy and healthy… for a time."

Pinching its brim between his fingers, Legba tipped his hat to Bones's sweetie, who held her severed head under her arm. "I wish knowing that made any of this easier."

I gave his arm a gentle squeeze. "I know it doesn't. I just need you to know you did the right thing by sending us away. And… I don't hold it against you."

Head tilting my way, shadows of sorrows past darkened his mismatched eyes. "Careful, child. That's beginning to sound like a goodbye. We can't give up before the fight has begun."

Lips pressed into a thin line, I rapidly blinked to keep the tears welling in my eyes at bay. "I wouldn't dream of it."

Legba tried to offer me a smile that in no way reached his eyes, when something at the front of the throne room snapped his attention that way. "Oh, no. My poor boy."

I followed his stare and joined my voice to one of the many gasps of shock that filled the room. Lugosi ambled in from a side door with Mel guiding him by the elbow. Dressed in a solid black tux, Lugosi's hair –which normally fell in stylish disarray—had been slicked back. The cosmetic glam he was known for had been wiped away to reveal deep, bruise-purple shadows under his eyes. His cheeks were gaunt, his lips gray. If I had to guess, Charlie fed him enough to keep him standing and little more.

Mel ushered Lugosi to the altar and lingered there long enough to ensure he could stand on his own. Fingertips brushing the small of his back, Mel mouthed the words *I love you* before returning to his station by the door with unchecked tears streaming down his cheeks.

"All of this is a love letter to Lugosi," I rasped, my voice breaking with emotion. "Charlie made Mel help in the planning simply to torture him. To spite her, he used every decoration and subtle nuance as a way to show Lugosi his love, even in the darkest hour of them being forced apart."

"To know a child of mine is capable of such cruelty breaks my heart." Legba shook a handkerchief from his pocket and handed it to me to dry my eyes.

Any response died on my lips as the music swelled, signaling it was time for the remaining guests to take a seat. With not enough chairs to accommodate, Legba and I stood with the crowd at the back of the throne room, lining the aisle. The band, which normally performed at the Afterlife Club, announced Charlie's entrance by strumming a punk melody of Beethoven's *Moonlight Sonata*. Out of equal parts fear and habit, all rose as the bride appeared.

Charlie was a vision, in a murderous sociopathic kind of way. A black beaded bodice hugged her limited curves to her hips, where it fanned out into layers of ruffled satin that cascaded to the floor like a moonlit waterfall. Holding a bouquet of purple and black roses, her hair was pinned up in a wreath of curls.

Walking her down the aisle with a victorious smirk was none other than The Friendly Houseguest. It seemed I'd underestimated my sister. The information he could deliver was more important to her than the handsome façade of which I'd robbed him.

Hands curling into fists at my sides, my fingers blackened with rage and rot.

Attuned to how I bristled, Legba tightened his hold on my arm. "We've come too far to lose control now," he whispered against my ear.

I managed a nod and nothing more.

March to the altar complete, Charlie handed her bouquet to The Guest while she adjusted the train of her gown, allowing her to turn and face the crowd. "Please, be seated," she purred, batting her lashes at her captive audience. "Not that any of you had a choice, but I'm honored you are all here to witness Lugosi and I exchanging the vows that will allow me to fully ascend in Legba power. Of course, not *everyone* could be with us tonight. Some plotted against me. Why, this very morning a foolish pair tried to break into the Dead End Resort to free those I had imprisoned!" she simpered. "Make no mistake, they were captured… and exorcised."

Catching hold of Legba's coat sleeve in a white-knuckled grip, warning sirens clanged through my mind. "Gideon… Bones…"

The words left my lips in a hushed whisper, yet Charlie's curls bobbed as her attention snapped my way. "Yes, dear sister, that includes that sexy piece of eye candy you've been sneaking around with. It's quite a pity. But, at least I have *you* here. So, what will it be? Willingly succeed the throne to me? Or launch into some lame ass, last-ditch effort to take back what never should have been yours in the first place?"

Shifting where they sat or stood, the audience glanced around in search of me.

I couldn't wait any longer.

The time to act had come.

Stepping away from Legba, I unhooked my mask and let it fall to the floor with the soft clink of metal. "It doesn't have to end in violence, Charlie. But it does have to end."

A chorus of shocked gasps and nervous energy filled the room, many of the residents looking at Charlie like a grenade with the pin pulled.

Lips pursing into a mock pout, she jabbed one fist onto her hip. "Does it, though? Because I know you weren't able to mark everyone with that nifty little symbol of yours. I can still make plenty of them hurt. In fact, if I'm feeling *threatened*, I could make them hack each other to pieces, just for fun. Would you like to walk through eternity with *that* on your conscience?"

Legba's journal explained that Charlie's heart was touched by death, a rot occurring within her that left her crippled to emotions or empathy. I could see it now. The sister I knew was gone, consumed by the empty void within her that no amount of power or privilege could ever fill. With that in mind, I lifted my chin and addressed the stranger before me. "I've hidden behind that mark for far too long, and so have you."

Giggling, she curled one bare shoulder inward, her hands fluttering to her neckline. "I couldn't agree more! How about if I slice yours off you and bring you around to my way of thinking?"

Stumbling in my momentary bravado, I glanced around the room. Faces I knew and loved peered back at me in hopeful expectation. There was no room for error. It all came down to this.

Chin dropping to my chest, the words soured on my tongue. "Are you sure you want to do this? We could leave our people with no one to lead them."

Charlie's head fell back, her booming laughter echoing to the rafters. "*That's* your plan? To inspire my sense of compassion by being utterly pathetic? I have to say, you disappoint me, Thadia. It's like you're not even trying."

I glanced up at her from under my brow, stabbing a murderous glare in her direction. "That's not my name… and I wasn't talking to you."

Sliding off his mask, Legba stepped forward and swept off his hat in a grand motion, standing tall to allow his people to drink him in.

Some uttered his name in breathy whispers.

Others openly wept tears of joy.

Those surrounding him reached out, longing to touch him.

All the while, Legba kept his stare locked on me. "They won't be alone. They'll have you."

At the time, I didn't know what he meant by that. But it caused shivers of unease to race down my spine.

"Who is that? What's happening?" Snatching her bouquet back from The Guest, Charlie dug her doll out from beneath the blooms. Funny, considering the real thing was hidden beneath the shoulder plate of my armor.

"That…" Eyes bulging in fear, The Houseguest shrank back towards the side door, "would be your father, King Legba Mortem."

"Crimson," Legba uttered the word as if sampling its flavor. "Your mother picked that name the day you were born because your lips were the color of freshly bloomed rose petals. Of course, when you returned to the land of the living, she renamed you in honor of her father, Charles."

Charlie wasn't really there.

She was an illusion cast by her own mind.

Still, shock managed to drain her complexion ashen. "No, that's not possible! You're dead."

Moving towards her with slow, steady strides, Legba offered her a disarming grin. "Comes with the territory, I'm afraid. A rather unavoidable demographic… for everyone but you."

"How? How is this possible?" Stumbling back a step, Charlie bumped into the altar. It swayed where it stood, threatening to topple over before Lugosi caught and steadied it.

"How is any of this?" With a flick of his wrist, Legba gestured to the room full of corpses. "It is all beyond our understanding, yet it is our actions that truly determine our fate. And for that, my beautiful child, I must apologize."

A valley of confusion sliced between her brows, Charlie pulled the pin from her torturous little doll. "Stay back!"

"I'm afraid that won't work on me," he explained with a sad smile. "As I was saying, I owe you an apology. I was selfish for bringing your mother here. Selfish to want the joy of family after wasting my former life. Still, I need you to know that everything I did, I did out of love. For all my children. Those I fathered, and those formed in my heart." Pausing, he pointedly glanced in Lugosi's direction. "Speaking of; hello, Lugosi. It is so good to see you, son."

Tears streamed down Lugosi's cheeks, his face crumpling into a mask of sorrow and regret. "Papa, I'm so—"

"Shh-shh-shh," Legba soothed in that deep, velvety timbre. "My regrets are many, but sacrificing myself for you isn't among them. I would do it a thousand times over. Because, sometimes, acts of love are as painful as they are worthwhile. Much like what I must do now." Stepping up on the altar beside Charlie, Legba closed his eyes and raised his hands to the heavens. "Spirits who surround, it is your favor I request. I call you to me now, from your place of rest."

Fires of rage simmered in the depths of Charlie's glare. "An exorcism? *Really*? There's a laundry list of reasons why that's a complete waste of time. However, it's good to see whose side you're on, *Father*." She spat the word with venomous hate, her scowl blaming me for his betrayal.

Smile widening, Legba's arms shot out to his sides. A blink morphed his eyes to a brilliant amethyst. Emerald flames ignited on his shoulders and licked down the lengths of his arms. "Follow my light. Be guided by my flame. Come to me now and ease… *the Rofenod's pain.*"

Bones cracked. Muscles tore. Shrieks echoed through the room as Legba took his monstrous form of the Rofenod one final time. No sooner was his transformation complete, than the white light of exorcism consumed him. His tendrils convulsed. That lone blue eye fixed and dilated as he stared oblivion in the face. As his soul was drawn into the glow, the beast was wrenched out first, momentarily leaving Legba behind. Legs buckling beneath him, he peered my way in peaceful resignation.

"Behold, the true Queen of Carnage Crossing." He smiled and extended a hand my way as his translucent form faded into nothingness. "In death may she reign."

NINETEEN

One final bolt of blinding light and the King was gone.

It took me a couple seconds to realize what had just happened. When Legba became the Rofenod, the Hamsa symbol was given even more protective potency. With him gone, it took away the power of the mark.

Charlie's slow clap broke the silence that fell, accompanied by a sharp whistle she blew through tightly pursed lips. "Well played, Thades. You convinced the King to off himself while his loyal subjects watched. You could have saved yourself some time by handing over the throne, but this was far more traumatizing for all parties involved. Bravo on that. However, with that hideous hand creature gone, I am left with one perplexing question." Holding her voodoo doll out in front of her, she swirled the pin around its torso as if hunting for the perfect spot to strike. "You have the mark, don't you? So, unless you just made a *monumentally* big mistake, this shouldn't work."

The pin stabbed into the chest of the doll, causing a white-hot pain to burrow into my heart and grind deep. Clutching one fist over my rib cage, I bent in half, catching myself with a hand on my knee.

"You don't have to be afraid of her." Forcing the words through a haze of pain, I pulled my secret weapon out from beneath my armor. "She showed us when she first arrived that she can't bring us all down at once. If we work together, we can take our town back. *This* is her voodoo doll. The real thing, not a conjuring connected to her metaphysical form. With a possession of hers, and candles burning all around, we can speak the words as Legba did and banish her soul from Carnage Crossing!"

Drawing the pin out, Charlie rammed it into the button-eye of her toy. "Why would they want to do that, Tempest?" she asked, tapping her fingernail on the head of the pin. "I brought life back to this desolate little wasteland. They can have an afterlife full of bountiful splendor thanks to *me*."

Feeling my skull was being split in two, I pressed the heels of my hands to my temples and began. "Spirits from the other side—"

That's as far as I got. Charlie pierced her pin inside the base of my spine, burying it to its head. Crashing to the ground, the doll slipped from my fingers and slid across the floor to bump the side of Enyo's jeweled slipper.

Without an ounce of hesitation, the culinary wizard picked it up and continued. "It is your favor I request."

"I command you to stop!" Charlie leveled Enyo with a throat jab of her metaphysical pin.

As an anguished scream tore from the chef's lungs, she tossed the doll to Malaria.

Chin jutting out, murder flashed behind the fashion designer's eyes. "I call you to me now—" Knifed in the gut, she doubled over, yet still managed to finish the verse. "—from your place of rest."

When being speared a second time silenced her, Azrael took over. "Follow the light."

Down he went.

Mina Foxglove dove in. "Be guided by its flame."

"You can't do this!" Charlie's face reddened with rage. "Don't you see? Your pitiful little island was dying without me. I brought back *life*! You do this, and you'll wither and rot like the corpses you are!"

Hope had been building, our community united for our common cause. Unfortunately, the memories of the rot that infected Carnage Crossing, threatening to reduce everything and everyone to dust, were too fresh to ignore. Not knowing if that destructive disease would return in Charlie's absence, my people—understandably—hesitated.

Feeling the shift in the dynamic, Charlie's heart-shaped lips curled into a victorious smirk. "That's right. For people who don't need to eat, the idea of actually starving and wasting away to bone is far from appealing, isn't it? Not to worry; I won't punish everyone for this display of insolence. Just those foolish enough to side with my sister's rotting reign."

Dragging myself up onto one knee, I crawled on trembling hands and knees to where the doll had fallen near the altar. I didn't know if I could make it, but I had to try. Gritting my teeth, I forced myself to push through the pain. It was the townhouse kitchen all over again, with Charlie administering merciless torture to further her twisted agenda.

It was that agonizing recollection that caused the answer to come crashing in with all the subtlety of a freight train.

The scene played on a loop behind my eyes.

Charlie, setting me up to be exorcised by Ambrose, her pins goring into me as her shouts echoed through my mind. "*Raise the Veil, Thades. Raise the Veil and this all goes away.*"

The Veil—although fractured—was in place, with Charlie's subconscious trapped on this side of it with us. That was a problem only I could fix. Tapping into the Legba magic coursing through my core, I rolled my fingers and awakened that green and purple charge that crackled down my arms.

Charlie's nervous gaze flicked in the direction of the growing glow emanating off me. "Stay down, Thades. You have to know you can't win this. Here, among these people, *I am a god*!"

A mighty pulse blasted from my chest, throwing my head back and curling my arms at my sides. Amethyst light exploded into the sky, peeling back what remained of the splintered Veil. Every person in the ballroom—minus my sputtering sister—morphed into the grisly, ghoulish forms of our decomposed earthly bodies. Think *Thriller*, but without the snappy choreography.

We might not have looked pretty… but we were free from the shackles of pain Charlie delivered.

Rigor stiff bodies ambled to their feet, moving in close to form a unified front of the dead and empowered.

Voice a gruff rasp, I focused my gray-eyed stare on my sister. "Take the hint, Charlie. We would rather wither in our divine decay than flourish in servitude to you."

My statement was punctuated by the stained-glass doors at the back of the room bursting open, allowing an iced-over Sparrow to shuffle in flanked by Gideon, Bones, Vesper, and Ember. Sure, they were all a party to my ghoulish brigade, with water spilling in torrents from Gideon's lips, black blood streaking Vesper's face, and icicles clinging to Sparrow's hair, but—bless Charlie's beating heart—for an instant she honestly believed she had gained back a measure of control.

Chin lifting to accommodate the weight of *my* crown, she stabbed a finger in my direction. "Seize my sister! Your Queen has spoken!"

Sparrow shuffled in, dragging one leg behind her. Ignoring Charlie's barked order, she retrieved the voodoo doll from where it landed.

"*No*!" An enraged shriek tearing from her throat, Charlie spun in her beautiful gown and shoved over the intricately constructed altar, sending it crashing to the ground in a flurry of foliage and kindling. "Why would you choose her over me? Look at the trees and growth I've brought back! She could never give you that!"

Each step looked agonizing as Sparrow hauled her locked limbs to the altar… and presented the doll to Lugosi. Handing over her offering, she kept her white-clouded gaze locked on my furious sibling. "Because under Tempest, *we are free.*" My lady-in-waiting turned her attention to Lugosi, the tendons in her neck popping with her efforts. "She was going to dictate your afterlife. It's only right you return the favor."

Charlie lunged forward, her extended hand intent on snatching the doll away. "I read the books! I did the research! Where there wasn't a way, *I made one*. I won't be taken down by glorified worm-fodder!"

Lugosi didn't back down, but faced her head-on. "Come to me now…" He glanced to Mel, offering him the final line of the incantation.

Tears of pride tangling with his lashes, Mel shook his head. "No, my love. It's only fitting that you finish it."

"You know what?" Hiking up the bottom hem of her gown, Charlie hopped from the altar and charged straight for me like a storm cloud of taffeta and lace. "Go for it. Do your worst. What do you think is going to happen? You saw my body. You know I'm not dead, and the living can't be exorcised. So, go ahead. Finish your stupid little rhyme. It won't touch me. *You* can't touch me."

Out of the corner of my eye, I watched Lugosi weigh the voodoo doll in his hand, seemingly deliberating over whether he was about to do more harm than good. Catching his eye, I granted him a nod of encouragement. "You're right, Charlie. I can't. But I *can* make sure you never step foot in Carnage Crossing again."

Chest puffed with purpose, Lugosi held the doll out in front of him and uttered the final words with impressive conviction for a corpse. "Let me ease Charlie's pain."

The blinding light that consumed Legba returned, enveloping my sister in a jarring current that locked her elbows and knees rigid. Thanks to her, I knew the exorcism process hurt like hell for the dead. Judging by the beads of sweat dotting her brow and the broken blood vessels blossoming on her cheeks, it wasn't a picnic for the living, either.

"This doesn't matter. Nothing you've done here does!" she spat, glaring my way with raw hatred. "I found my way beyond the Veil once. I'll do it again. After all, I've still got Mom's journals. Pity you didn't grab those along with the doll."

I strolled towards her without an ounce of contempt, knowing her time hurting my people had come to an end. "And I have Dad's. You remember him? The tall guy you met in passing? He harnessed the power of the Veil, as I can, and you never will. What you fail to realize, little sister, is that *he* was the one who came up with the first exorcism to banish souls found to be too dangerous or destructive to stay in Carnage Crossing. Once these words have been spoken over a soul, they can never step foot here again. The only exception being our father. Unfortunately for you, he took the details of that little loophole with him." Reaching my hand into that coursing light, I placed my palm on Charlie's cheek. My skin flaked away, tissue turning to dust by the powerful flow of coursing energy. Still, I maintained the connection to say a final goodbye to my only sister. "From here, you'll go back to your life and live until your dying day…whenever that may be. Even then, you won't return here. Change your ways, and you might just join Mom at the top of that great escalator in the sky."

While Charlie's form began to fade, her spirit wrestled with what she still couldn't accept. "And if I don't? If I make it my life's purpose to find my way back here and bring you down?"

Pulling my hand out of the light, I took a step back to inject an eternity of distance between us. "Then, little sister, you… *will*… burn."

One final, blinding flash and Charlie vanished with a furious scream.

All that remained where she stood was my crown spinning to a stop in the space she vacated.

TWENTY

Centering my energy, I sealed the Veil shut and returned us all to our ghoulishly fabulous selves. Unfortunately, for the island at least, it wasn't enough. Black fissures still splintered the skyline, leaving the Veil cracked and distorted. The silence that fell was broken by the heels of Malaria's shoes clicking across the floor to retrieve my crown where it fell.

Flipping her hair back to expose the charred side of her face, she lifted her voice to fill the room. "I don't believe you ever had the coronation intended for you, My Queen."

My eyes narrowed, anticipating a snarky comment to follow. "And you think *now* is the ideal time for that?"

Brows raised, she slapped me with a dose of her brutal honesty. "I believe it's your job to fix the Veil. No time like the present, unless you'd like to wait for something worse than your sister to wriggle its way in?"

"When you put it like that..." What began as my casual stride across the room quickly shifted. Each resident took a knee as I passed, clapping their fists over their stilled hearts.

From somewhere in the crowd, a single soul called out, "In death may she reign."

It awoke a chorus of voices that filled the cavernous room, lifting to the rafters. "In death may she reign. *In death may she reign*!"

Reaching the front of the throne room, I faced my people and knelt. The chains of my gown clapped together with the motion, seemingly applauding the night's victory. As Malaria lowered the crown to my head, tears of joy welled behind my eyes and blurred my vision. These people, this eclectic group of misfits, were more than my subjects, neighbors, and friends. They were family. Whatever I had done in life, whatever successes or failures led me here, I thanked Legba for every single moment. Because it all allowed me to find my way home.

No sooner did the much-missed weight of my crown settle on my head, than a pulse of energy tore from my core. Arms flung out at my sides, my head fell back as a geyser of emerald and amethyst coursed from my essence, sealing every crack in the Veil and binding every fracture. Only when it was restored, allowing the Northern Lights to shimmer and dance across the skyline in all their mesmerizing beauty, did my magic retract and a hush fall.

Behind me, Malaria cleared her throat to hide an uncharacteristic quiver of emotion. "Rise, Tempest Mortem, rightful heir to the throne of Legba."

Thunderous applause erupted, my people rising in joyous celebration.

Striding up the aisle, Gideon offered me a hand to help me to my feet. "Thanks to you, the people of Carnage Crossing can once again enjoy their afterlives, *mo bhanrion*. How shall we celebrate?"

Flicking a rogue lock of hair from my eyes, I glanced in Lugosi's direction. Not that he noticed. He and Mel were locked in a much-needed embrace. "It would be a shame for anyone to leave when we were all brought here with the promise of a wedding."

At that, Lugosi's head snapped my way. "Really? You would…? We can…?"

Fighting off a grin, I offered a dismissive shrug. "That's for the grooms to decide, not me."

Putting an arm's distance between him and his betrothed, Lugosi bit his lower lip, trying—and failing miserably—not to appear too excited about the prospect. "What do you say? I know the last few days have been miserable, but we could put all of this behind us and move forward… together."

In a truly magnificent performance that even put Vesper to shame, Mel managed to keep his expression stoic and unreadable. "I will consider it, under *one* condition."

Eyebrows lifting to his hairline, silver sparks of hope swirled in Lugosi's eyes. "Anything. Name it."

"What I want," unbuttoning the stuffy black coat Charlie forced him into, Mel shrugged it off and folded it over his arm, "is to shake any of Charlie's influences off of this wedding and make it our own. Think we can do that?"

Cradling Mel's face between his palms, Lugosi pressed his forehead to that of his soon-to-be husband's. "I do… with a little bit of help."

At that, the couple turned their questioning gazes to the townspeople.

"*Praise Legba*! We're going to make *this* the wedding Carnage Crossing deserves!" Immediately, Malaria snapped her fingers three times over her head. "Sparrow, move all the lanterns up front and arrange them around the altar. Bones, those evergreens need to be in here lining the aisle. Those remind Mel of his Gizmo, and she should be represented on his special day."

"I have a Gizmo?" Mel whispered in confusion, rightfully afraid to interrupt the barked commands of the focused fashion designer.

"It's her word for *grandma*." Ruffling his fingers through his hair, Lugosi returned his bold green locks to their normal state of stylish disarray.

"I'm stealing some roses from the crumbled altar, and the sticks and pine from the back of these chairs." Enyo's fingers worked to free them from the fabric they were knotted in. "That wedding cake needs a bit of afterlife flare."

"Fantastic! Ember and Vesper, you clear away the rest of the altar rubble while I get started on giving these boys the fashion upgrade they deserve." When I side-stepped out of the way of the buzzing activity, Malaria jabbed a finger in my direction. "Don't venture too far, Your Highness. I'm using the armor on your dress for parts."

"I wouldn't dream of it," I chuckled, stepping closer to Gideon as Ember and Vesper dragged out the largest piece of the destroyed altar behind us.

Pressing a kiss to my temple, Gideon lowered his voice for my ears only. "Sweet as this is, there's more to this. You're keeping us all here for a reason. What's up?"

Linking my arm with his, I led him to the side wall. I was about to begin my explanation when Azrael inserted himself into the conversation. Charming smile in place and my father's makeshift jewel still rammed in his eye socket, he politely waited for me to continue. Shaking off the odd intrusion, I pressed on. "The Friendly Houseguest vanished. Much of the information Charlie had, he supplied her with. The guy plotted against me and is now trying to disappear. Seeing as he can travel through the walls, I don't want him to get far. While everyone is distracted with redesigning the wedding, I need you to search the manor and find him."

Hands folded in front of him, Azrael's lips parted with a pop. "Not sure that directive was meant for me. I simply didn't want to interrupt. Question: following the couple's first dance, should I cover an Ed Sheeran song or something from the Maroon Five catalog?"

I blinked in his direction. Once, and then again. "You're a part of this now. Find him!"

Seeing Gideon was already striding from the room, Azrael turned on his heel to follow him. "Yes, Your Highness."

"Oh, and Azrael?" I called after him. "Sheeran. Always go with Sheeran."

TWENTY-ONE

The spectacle of gothic beauty spilled out of the throne room and into the ballroom. Black linens draped every table, a gorgeous assortment of black and white roses nestled in the center of each. Beside each arrangement sat a skull wearing a crown of small pink and white flowers. The rose petals that could be salvaged from the smashed altar led out the reception area and down the aisle to where Mel and Lugosi stood before me.

At Malaria's insistence, Lugosi lost his shirt and tie. Clad in his tuxedo jacket with nothing underneath, the shoulder plates of my armored ensemble were gifted to him to add a bold, sexy edge to his sleek glamor. Mel's look tiptoed more on the side of subtlety. His bow tie was gone, the top two buttons of his shirt undone. The solid black jacket Charlie insisted upon had been replaced with one tailored out of a silver, satin brocade.

As a lone pianist played a haunting melody of Fleetwood Mac's "Rhiannon", Mel and Lugosi came before the entire town that had rallied together to make their special day possible.

Stripped of the pageantry of my gown's former metal accents, I presided over vows in the silver chainmail slip I'd worn underneath my former gown. Clearing my throat, I began. "Mel, Lugosi, no one in this room can begin to fathom what you've been through these last few days. Through it all, you supported each other any way you could, even when doing so meant breaking your own heart. It may sound strange to say, yet those of us who observed your mutual selflessness in the face of these unfathomable odds consider ourselves lucky… because we know we witnessed true, unbreakable love. The kind that will look eternity in the face and know… it's still not long enough." Voice cracking, I dropped my chin to my chest to fight off a sniffle of emotion.

Snapping a handkerchief from his pocket, Lugosi passed it to me. "Girl, you better stop before I start." His voice betrayed him by quivering. "I'm looking fine as hell, and you know I'm an ugly crier."

"Fair enough," I giggled through my tears. "How about if we move to the part where you take Mel's hand."

"Gladly." He did so without hesitation, pausing to dot a quick kiss between Mel's knuckles.

Placing both of my hands over theirs, I called forth a shimmering shroud of emerald and amethyst to cocoon the couple. "Repeat after me: we will share each other's pain and seek to ease it."

While both men repeated the phrase, the words lodged in Mel's voice with a lump of emotion he swallowed hard to speak around. Lugosi encouraged his love by rubbing the one thumb he still had in small circles over the back of Mel's hand.

"We join in our burdens and battle them in this union." As I uttered the second sentiment, my gaze sought Gideon out in the crowd. The vows the couple were pledging to one another were the same the dashing pirate and I once spoke to one another on the deck of his ship.

The look he graced me with in response was one of undeniable devotion.

Fingers tightly entwined, the couple echoed the sentiment.

Retracting the shroud, I dropped my hands to my sides. "Do you have the rings?"

"Oh!" Mel chirped, only to immediately cringe and shrink away from his own enthusiasm. "About that. I had an idea. It seemed cute at the time. Now, I'm kind of regretting going for it."

In the middle of retrieving Mel's silver band from the pocket inside his jacket, Lugosi hesitated. "That's ominous. What did you do?"

"Uh… remember when rot overtook the island and your thumb fell off?"

Lugosi's brow creased, a smile tugging at the corner of his lips as he wiggled his nub. "Hard thing to forget."

Gnawing on his lower lip, Mel pulled a small black satchel out of his pocket. "You're either going to find this adorable… or horrifying."

Turning his hand palm up, he revealed Lugosi's severed thumb with a gold band slid up to the knuckle.

A bark of laughter escaping him, Lugosi clapped both hands over his mouth. "Can it be both? Because this is a special kind of twisted, you beautiful little freak!"

Watching Mel extract the thumb and retrieve the ring, I couldn't help but chuckle. When the two were ready, I fed them the next verse. "With this bound hand, I will lift your sorrows and light your path with my steadfast devotion."

While they exchanged their rings, my stare sought out Gideon once more. Ocean-blue gaze locking with mine, he mouthed the same declaration to me. How was it my heart had stopped beating long ago, yet never felt full and content until now?

I finished binding the two men together with the words, "From now until the very end of my eternity, this is my vow."

Blinking back tears, both choked out the words in raspy whispers. "From now until the very end of my eternity, this… is my vow."

"In Legba's name, I pronounce you wed. In death shall you forever be united." Looking to Lugosi, I jerked my head in Mel's direction. "Why don't you give him a kiss?"

Onlookers erupted in applause as the couple's lips met in a passionate explosion. Keeping their foreheads together, both men laughed at the joy they found against all odds before hooking arms and leading the crowd into the ballroom.

There we were welcomed by Azrael, who clanked a spoon on the side of his champagne glass from his position in front of the band. "All right, you two. Save the sappy stuff for the honeymoon." Laughter rippled through the room. "Speaking of which, I have a special suite and some deluxe spa treatments waiting for you at the Dead End Resort and Day Spa—my treat in honor of your special day."

Polite applause.

"But now," Azrael gave a nod to the drummer, who built anticipation with a steady drumroll, "Lennox, from the Afterlife Club, opened the bar in the corner. Enyo has a table of wickedly delightful treats. So, let's get this party started!" The music rose and Azrael launched into a booming rendition of Freddy Mercury's "Love Me Like There's No Tomorrow".

The grooms took their place on the dance floor, swaying in each other's embrace.

Finding Gideon by the bar, I bumped his elbow with mine. "Any luck?"

The pirate thanked Lennox for the two fingers of rum with a nod. "No sign of him. Wherever he disappeared to, he's not in the manor. One way or another, I'm sure he'll show up. Conniving creeps like him gravitate to trouble. But in the meantime…" Catching my elbow, he turned me to face the reception. "In case you missed it, there seems to be a party going on. Not sure if you noticed. That being the case, why don't we let ourselves celebrate today's win?" My mouth opened to protest, only for Gideon to make a convincing argument by kissing his way down my neck. "This is far from the end. Eternity stretches out before us. Make no mistake, we will face other oddities and threats. But look at this unruly band of misfits. Whatever dares come our way won't stand a chance."

As his hands snaked around my waist, I let my stare sweep over the mingling residents.

Bones and his headless girlfriend joined the newlyweds on the dance floor, both couples twirling and spinning in an elegant waltz.

Enyo sliced a piece of red velvet wedding cake for Malaria, who twitched her finger and winked for Enyo to throw on some extra frosting.

Lennox flipped a bottle of Scotch over the back of her hand and poured a shot directly into the mouth of Mina Foxglove.

Ember and Sparrow doubled over in laughter as Vesper joined Azrael for a chorus—each man trying to top the other with a better Freddy Mercury impression.

My people.

No longer did I see the traces of death that marred each of them.

All I saw was… family.

"Death couldn't stop one person here," I chuckled with a shake of my head.

"It's hard to imagine anything that could." Turning me to face him, Gideon pulled me close.

Peering up at him, I brushed his chiseled jawline with the tip of my nose. "What do you say, sailor? Want to make this thing official and move in here with me?"

Sucking air through his teeth, he attempted a cringe that was made far less convincing by the amusement crinkling the corners of his eyes. "Live with my wife? I don't know, isn't that a bit conventional for us?"

"Well, if you'd rather remain glorified pen pals…"

I tried to pull away, only for him to tighten his hold. "*Mo bhanrion*, there is nothing I'd like more than to spend my eternity with you."

My lips teased over his without offering the sweet release of contact. "Is that a yes?"

Hands at my hips, Gideon lifted me from the ground and claimed my lips with his. "That's a *hell* yes."

Head falling back with a giggle, I caught my crown with one hand. "Like *all* the moments like this that have come before, I do need to point out that we—once again—have an audience. A rather large one, in fact."

Easing my feet to the ground, my pirate hooked his finger beneath my chin and raised my mouth to his. "Let them look. There isn't a person here who doesn't know our story has a happy ending... all because of you."

Our lips met in a delicious promise of passion to come.

Reservations abandoned, we joined the others in uproarious celebration.

Singing.

Dancing.

Food.

Booze.

In that moment, all was well in our ghoulishly glamorous town.

Or... so we thought.

How could we know that while the entire reception was coming together for a rousing chorus of "Total Eclipse of the Heart", The Friendly Houseguest was traveling through the walls of the town to the Home DeadPot? Whistling a merry tune, he sauntered through the empty warehouse to the booth of the one being occupying the space. Parting the heavy curtains, he sauntered into The Host's space and clicked on the television set. Folding his hands in front of him, he waited as the glow of static illuminated the screen.

A shadowy, bulbous head rose from behind the television as voice clips crackled from the speakers.

"Welcome."

"This is..."

"The host with the most."

"Whom do you seek?"

Ignoring the rule to keep his eyes on the screen, The Houseguest paced around the set, taking special note of how The Host's spindly limbs curled around it. "I didn't come for answers or insight into prophetic concerns. Those matters are for those still clinging to their humanity. I come… with a proposition."

Irritated that its rules weren't being abided by, The Host let a menacing hiss seep through its teeth.

"Obey the rules."

"Drive safely."

"… Or die!"

Clucking his tongue against the roof of his mouth, The Houseguest continued on course. Planting himself in front of the TV, he peered at the screen to appease his potential partner. "There's no need to get cranky, friend. You and I are one and the same. Monsters tamed to play nice. Even now, here we are hiding in the darkness while the rest of the town joins together in a jovial celebration. Yet when things get truly bad, who is it they call upon?"

A crackle of static. Then, *"You and me…"*

"Face to face."

"That's right. We have foresight and abilities they can't even fathom. Still, they cast us aside and dismiss us. This very night, the Queen was almost overthrown. I saw how it happened. Made note of every flaw. That is how you and I will succeed where others have failed."

"State the answer in the form of a question."

"Trust me with your truth."

The Houseguest's gray lips twisted into a malicious smile. "I am drawn to power by a magnetic pull. Tonight, I sensed it in a raw, untapped form. Darkness courses through the veins of one unaware of the true nature of their own sinister lineage. We could mold her. Manipulate her. And allow a new day to dawn… of monsters and mayhem."

"What is in a name?"

"Speak!"

The Houseguest dragged his tongue across his top teeth, reveling in how The Host hung on his every word. "Her name… is Malaria Cain."

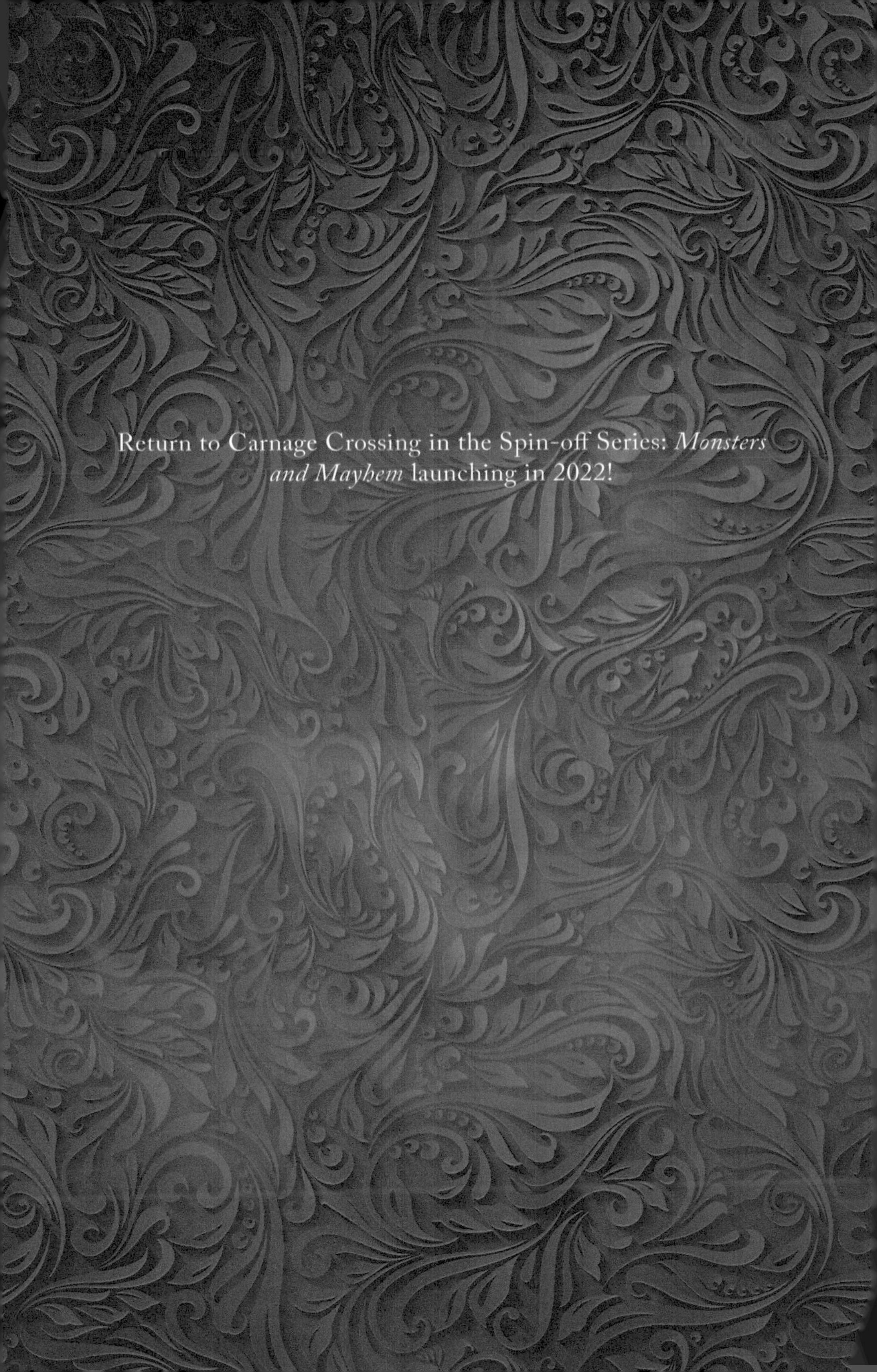

Return to Carnage Crossing in the Spin-off Series: *Monsters and Mayhem* launching in 2022!

ABOUT THE AUTHOR

PennedCon Award Winner Author of the Year 2020
PennedCon Award Winner Best Book Blurb 2020
TopShelf Award Winner Best Science Fiction 2019
Utopia Award Winner Author of the Year 2018
Utopia Award Winner for Best Villain 2018 for Ursela in Rise of the Sea Witch
Readers' Favorite YA Fantasy Bronze Medal Winner 2017
Readers' Favorite Fantasy Silver Medal Winner for 2015
Turning Pages Magazine Winner for Best YA book of 2013 & Best Teen Book of 2013
RONE Award Winner for Best YA Paranormal Work of 2012
Young Adult and Teen Reader voted Author of the Year 2012

Stacey Rourke is the award-winning author of works that span genres but possess the same flare for fast-paced action and snarky humor. She lives in Florida with her husband, two beautiful daughters, and two spoiled rotten dogs. Stacey loves to travel, is obsessed with all things Disney, and considers herself blessed to make a career out of talking to the imaginary people that live in her head.

Connect with her at:
www.staceyrourke.com
Facebook at www.facebook.com/staceyrourkeauthor
Amazon Author Page: http://amzn.to/2l8FlbH
or Instagram @rourkewrites

OTHER TITLES BY STACEY ROURKE

THE GRYPHON SERIES

The Conduit
Embrace
Sacrifice
Ascension

THE LEGENDS SAGA

Crane
Raven
Steam

REEL ROMANCE

Adapted for Film
Turn Tables

TS901 CHRONICLES

Co-written with Tish Thawer
TS901: Anomaly
TS901: Dominion

VEILED SERIES

Veiled
Vlad
Vendetta

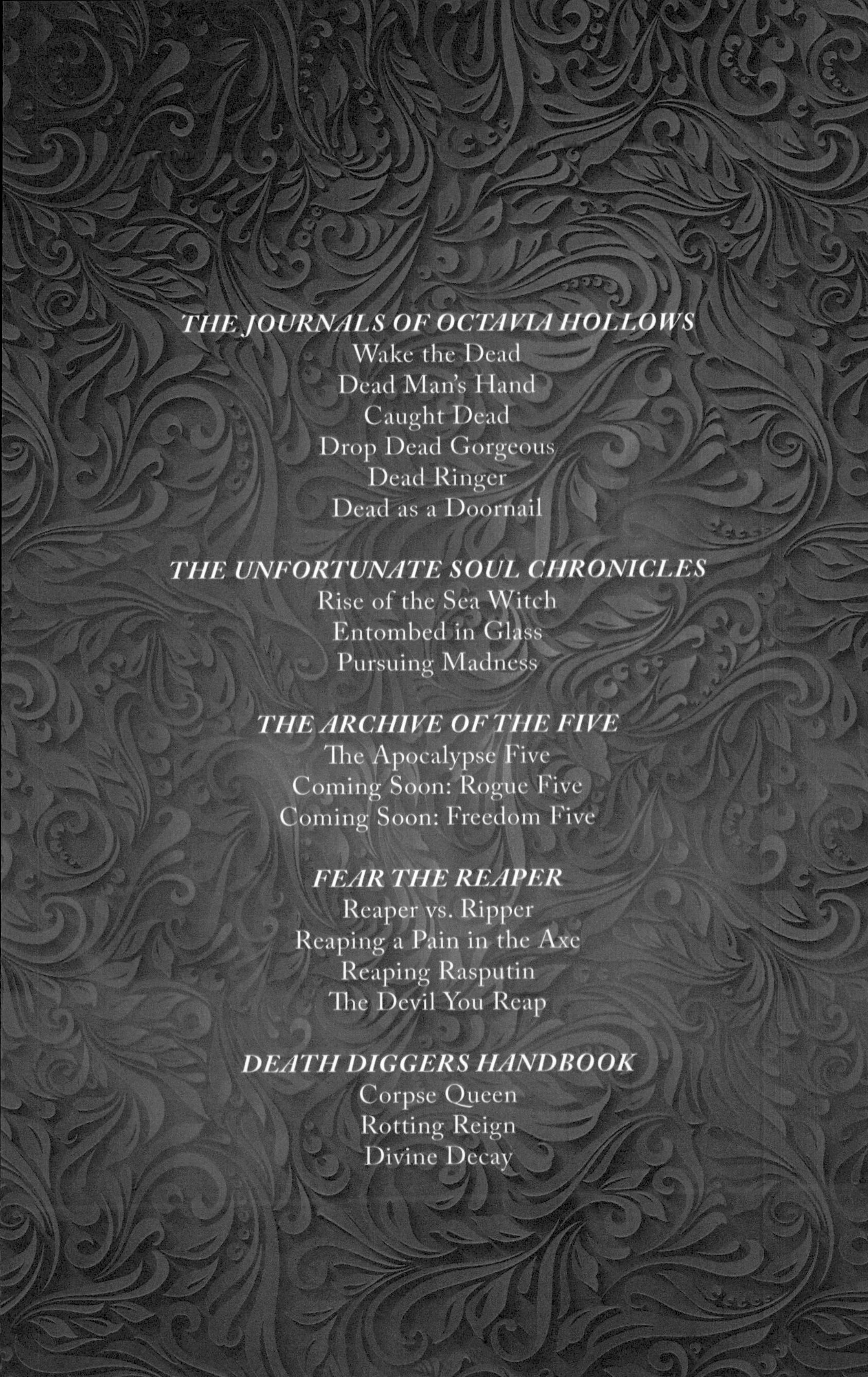

THE JOURNALS OF OCTAVIA HOLLOWS
Wake the Dead
Dead Man's Hand
Caught Dead
Drop Dead Gorgeous
Dead Ringer
Dead as a Doornail

THE UNFORTUNATE SOUL CHRONICLES
Rise of the Sea Witch
Entombed in Glass
Pursuing Madness

THE ARCHIVE OF THE FIVE
The Apocalypse Five
Coming Soon: Rogue Five
Coming Soon: Freedom Five

FEAR THE REAPER
Reaper vs. Ripper
Reaping a Pain in the Axe
Reaping Rasputin
The Devil You Reap

DEATH DIGGERS HANDBOOK
Corpse Queen
Rotting Reign
Divine Decay

www.ingramcontent.com/pod-product-compliance
Ingram Content Group UK Ltd.
Pitfield, Milton Keynes, MK11 3LW, UK
UKHW041639190726
13854UKWH00006B/2595

9 798767 509980